UNEARTHING GAIA

PALDIMORI GODS RISING

T.L. CALLAHAN

DRAGON MOUNTAIN
PRESS

First published in United States of America by Dragon Mountain Press LLC 2018

1

Callahan, T.L. Unearthing Gaia: Paldimori Gods Rising 2

PB ISBN: 978-0-9991225-9-4
EB ISBN: 978-0-9991225-3-2

Edited by Book Nanny Writing and Editing Services

Cover design by: Covers by Juan
Artwork by: janko_m

Publisher: Dragon Mountain Press LLC, 1250 W. Ohio Pike # 199 Amelia, OH 45102

❦ Created with Vellum

ALSO BY T.L. CALLAHAN

For the small but mighty Callahan Clan.
Your support and feedback mean the world to me.

PROLOGUE

"Kinky isn't a crime! Lia shouldn't do the time!"

I marched back and forth in front of the police station where my best friend was being held behind bars and thrust my sign in the air. *Mr. Skittles Says Free Lia or You'll Find his Rainbow in Your Shoes*, it read. The crowd were giving me weird looks and I had to explain my cat had inherited my obsession with Skittles. He coughed up rainbow hair balls. They didn't think it was funny, but Lia would have gotten it. I missed her.

The sun blasted down from its peak in the sky heating the parking lot under my feet until my sandals felt like they were melting. Sweat beaded my forehead. The alcohol I'd downed last night seeped from my pores in a nauseating sour-sweet smell. Luckily, the breeze was one thing you could count on when living in Washington. As a sudden wind whipped my long hair around me, it brought a moment of welcome relief.

The crowd gathered on the sidewalk buzzed with gossip, but I ignored them all. The tension in this town had been building for a while: the gossip turning more vicious, fights getting more frequent. I wasn't sure when it had started, but our normally placid little town was on a witch hunt. Unfortunately, they thought Lia was the witch.

All of that weird stuff people were saying she did—it was all a lie. I knew my friend. Ever since we'd been a couple of sleep-starved college freshman doing manual labor by bringing the seniors their donuts. One massive collision had resulted in donut casualties all round and a lifelong friendship. As for the kinky sex stuff—well, that was no one's business but hers. Not that I thought my straightlaced friend was into that either.

I'd had my share of runs through the rumor mill having grown up in Port Lawson, but nothing like what my bestie had been through over the last couple of months. Even the thought of the things she was accused of made me sick. If I hadn't already had my stomach pumped at the hospital this morning, last night's dinner of salad and donuts would have been making a reappearance.

I'd gotten the SOS drunken phone call from Lia on her way home from the airport last evening and had been waiting on her apartment steps with chocolate when she arrived back. She'd jumped from the back of a black Lexus before it came to a stop and was ugly-crying on my shoulder before I could say hello. A guy in a pilot uniform got out of the Lexus and, cussing at her recklessness, grabbed Lia's arm before she toppled us both onto the driveway. He introduced himself as Captain Jack Mathews, a pair of sexy dimples framing his amused smile. Lia had insisted it was a girl's night in and we were raiding her stash of alcohol. The captain had declared us trouble and appointed himself as our babysitter.

The alcohol flowed as Lia told me about the tropical island paradise where she had gone to compete in that mysterious game. Most people would have picked up a souvenir like a shell necklace, but *she*, apparently, had picked up a stalker. The details were sketchy. Most of the time she had ranted about some guy named Bennett, who was the biggest a-hole she'd ever met. I let her talk and cry it out. My own worries about Dan's weird behavior lately seemed small in comparison.

Everything after that was a blur. I'd woken up in the captain's shirt with a red-faced policeman hovering over me. His much nicer partner had escorted me—under protest—into the back of an ambulance. Now here I was. A one-woman picket line defending Lia's innocence and sexual preferences for all.

"Free Lia!" I shouted and spun on my heel.

And slammed into a solid wall of muscle. Tresses of hair flew into my face. Pink feathers slipped loose from their clips and fluttered to the ground. The scent of spiced wine filled my nose making me lean closer to the warm chest underneath my palm for a better sniff.

"Are you molting?" A velvety smooth voice traced down my spine like a caress.

I pushed my hair back and looked up into midnight-blue eyes full of laughter. The wind gusted and pushed me against the man's solid frame. His lips tipped in a devilish smile that set off a tremor in my body like an earthquake.

My overly active brain started firing off random thoughts. *Pretty. Tell him he can help you shed a few layers. We don't talk to strangers. Look at those lips! No one likes a forward woman.*

His smile slipped a little as I continued to stare at him. I shook my head, as if I could physically dislodge my thoughts, and took a step back. "Hi. Hey. Uh ..."

"If you're looking for another way to greet me, 'What's

up?' would definitely apply," He grinned and pushed his shoulder-length wavy blonde hair back out of his face. "Jaxon Baines. And you are?"

"Dia King."

"A unique name for a unique lady," he said in a husky voice that sent another tremor through me. His hand covered mine where I had been absentmindedly rubbing his chest. "You can pet me all night long if you want, sweetheart. I'll be sure to return the favor."

I was mesmerized by those sinfully plump lips as they formed every word. The world around us had ceased to exist. All I could hear was the ever-present noise in my head. The hum of activity, like a thousand buzzing bees, and the random thoughts that peppered me with too much information. *Get closer. Run away. His eyes look like deep ocean pools. Talking to strange men is a bad idea. Did he proposition me? I don't see a wedding band. Why is he wearing a suit? Grab that tie and reel him in for a kiss!*

He was still talking. "I'm staying at Vern's Hotel. Room nineteen."

I blinked in confusion for a moment, wondering if I had heard him correctly. Great Mother have mercy, he went right for the mattress mambo invite.

He chuckled, breaking the spell, and heat crept across my chest. I'd never reacted like this before to any man—not even Dan. I jerked my hand away and put more distance between us. He smirked, like he knew exactly what he was doing to me.

"Wow, you're really forward. I mean, I've met a few guys like you, but usually they at least want to buy me a drink first. Not that that works either. The free drink is nice, though. I'm just saying you may want to warm a girl up before going straight to 'Hey baby, want to come back to my hotel room.'"

"For the record, I didn't say it like that." His hot gaze scanned over my Little Mermaid tank top that said: *Today is Leg Day.* The smirk was back as his eyes dipped down to my less-than-impressive chest and stopped to take inventory. I gave it a minute—guys seemed to be fascinated when you don't wear a bra, no matter the size. His eyes, when they met mine again, promised that he appreciated the view and planned to show me just how much.

Lust bloomed in my core so quickly my knees wobbled. He twirled one of the feathers that had fallen from my hair between his fingers. Then brushed it against my cheek.

"But I don't believe in denying my desires. Why waste time with games when there is so much more we could be doing? I bet we can put this feather to good use."

"Uh huh, ok then." I took a ragged breath, trying to ignore the mental image of him trailing that feather down my naked body. *You have a boyfriend. Remember Dan, the guy you plan to marry?* "I mean, that is totally out of line. I'm not looking to hook up with you."

"Technically I wasn't looking for a 'hook-up' either. Then I bumped into you and my plans changed. I would love to see this beautiful hair spread across my pillow."

He twined a lock of my hair around his finger and leaned down to place his lips next to my ear. I gulped heavily, my heart beating as fast as a humming bird's wings.

"Mmm ..." he said, "... you smell like strawberry shortcake. I bet you taste just as sweet." He brushed the feather down to dip into the scooped neck of my shirt. His warm breath fanned across my ear as he said, "I'm very curious to see if the rest of your body is this same golden color all over."

The next thing I knew my picket sign had whacked him on the head. Down Jaxon Baines went. I don't know which of us was most surprised. He looked up at me, his face a comical mask of shock and awe. Pink glitter in the shape of a paw print stuck to his cheek where the sign had struck him. More glitter fluttered through the air coating his hair and suit.

He shielded his eyes, giving me a once-over. "Good gods, you're like a psychedelic pint-sized menace-to-society."

"Oh, thanks! Glad to know I'm sending the right message."

Jaxon Baines threw back his head and laughed. Great Mother, he was the most beautiful man I'd ever seen. Then the wind gusted, nearly knocking me on top of him. It whipped around him, like in a wind tunnel, brushing the glitter from him.

His laughter died as he got to his feet. He opened his mouth to say something but was cut off as several women rushed to his side. They fussed over him offering to help him in any way possible while shooting scowls at me. I knew at least one of those women was married but, there they were, flirting away. Unbelievable. Jaxon gave me a wicked little smile that said, "See, works on everyone but you."

My gaze dropped to the ground as an old familiar pain knifed through me. It was stupid to feel like this. To feel like an outsider, always different. I didn't want to be one of those women who threw themselves at men. But the looks they'd given me brought me right back to my childhood. When I was the dirty gypsy girl or the poor kid whose mom was crazy.

You choose your happiness, Dia. It doesn't matter what they think.

I notched my chin in the air and raised my sign. I had

my teaching career. I had Dan, and we were going get married and start a family one day soon. I had my best friend Lia. What else could I want? Jaxon was a flirt who was used to getting women to fall into his bed. I wouldn't be caught off guard again.

One of the women giggled and clung to Jaxon's arm. I straightened my spine. *It is your civic duty to clue these women in to the walking hormone factory and his nefarious intentions.*

"Ladies, don't be fooled by the pretty face. He's the wham-bam-don't-call-me kind." Jaxon frowned at me—when I finally looked at him again. "You deserve better."

They all stared at me in confusion.

"Ladies, I'm fine." Jaxon jumped in to break the awkward silence. He somehow extracted himself from the women's clutches. A dazzling smile crossed those sinful lips and I could almost hear the IQ levels drop. It was a shock to the system how quickly he could turn on the charm. He was a danger to women's sanity. "I hate to rush off, but I'm actually late for an appointment. Thank you for your concern."

"Oh, are you here on business?" one of the women asked.

"Will you be in town long?" another asked. "I can be your tour guide."

"I'm Lia Davies' lawyer." Jaxon picked up his briefcase and about a dozen women ogled his butt. He answered the woman, but his gaze was on me. "I can't say how long I'll be around. I wouldn't mind someone showing me the best spots for food in town, though."

The women started arguing over who would be his guide. I counted down the seconds to disaster. There was the screeching. Yep, the hair pulling. Oh wow, that was an elbow to the stomach. I sighed as the tangle of women hit the blacktop. And this is why I needed to warn them. Hurricane Jaxon was here and was going to rock this town.

Jaxon eased around the fighting women toward the police department door.

"Hey, wait," I called out, just before he could slip inside. He turned with that megawatt smile in place, but it slipped when he saw that it was me. The irritating grin came back out.

"Did you change your mind about the wham-bam-don't-call-me night of fun?" he asked, amused.

"Not happening." I glared at him. "I want you to stay away from the women in this town."

"What makes you think they'll stay away from me?" he asked, looking truly curious. "I hate to break it to you, little peacock, but those women aren't looking for anything more than a good time either."

What had he called me? Gah! He was so annoying.

And he was wrong about those women. They might say they were fine with a hook-up, but most of them would still be thinking they could be the one. The one woman who could change him and make him stay. That all he needed was the right woman to love him. I'd seen those women and the devastation that came when it didn't work. Women like my mother.

"I'm not going to let you leave a trail of broken hearts in my town." I set the sign on my shoulder menacingly. "You're here to do a job. Lia is my best friend. She didn't do whatever they're saying. If you don't get her out of there, mister hotshot lawyer, I'm going to bedazzle the inside of your underwear."

1

AUGUST

A group of little expectant faces looked back at me across the classroom as I leaned against my desk. I took a deep breath, savoring the waxy smell of crayons mixed with the fruity scents of our last project of homemade finger paints. Brightly colored cabinets and bins filled with assorted art supplies lined the back wall. A sink stood in one corner next to a row of little art smocks hanging on pegs. Paper lanterns swayed in the breeze from the air conditioner vents on the ceiling. Nearly every available surface was covered with the art projects from my classes over the last three years at W.C. Lawson Academy.

My classroom was more of a home to me than the house I was living in with Dan. Every scrap of art in this room was an outlet for a child's imagination that I had helped to nurture. It filled me with pride and made me giddy all over again that I had gotten this teaching position at one of the best schools in the area. I'd built up this classroom to be my paradise: the place where I could truly be me.

"Cats," Mia shouted from the table toward the back of the room.

"Let's raise our hands, ok?" I gave her a wink and she giggled. "One of the other classes already picked cats."

"How about ponies, Ms. Dia?" Rachel asked with her hand in the air, her golden-brown pigtails swinging as she kicked her feet.

I tilted my head letting the image of horses prancing across fluffy white clouds take form. My artistic soul appreciated the image, but it didn't feel right. And I always trusted my instincts when it came to art. "Hmm, good suggestion, but maybe we can think of some other ideas."

Each class was to pick their theme for the kites we would make for our festival in a couple of weeks. The other classes had already started on theirs, but this class was still struggling to find their theme. Inspiration had struck last year when I had dragged Dan along with me on a five-hour drive down the coast to Long Beach to witness the awesomeness of tens of thousands of kites soaring at the International Kite Festival. It had been so amazing that I had decided that Port Lawson would have our own little version of those festivities this year. Now we just had to pull it all together.

"Yeah, cuz it's dumb," Ronnie groaned. "You always wanna make horses. How 'bout the Indominus Rex like in *Jurassic World*? He would eat all the other kites. RAWWR, RAWWR. Chomp."

"Ronnie it's not nice to call things dumb." I struggled to keep the irritation out of my voice. "This is a friendly competition. We don't want to eat the other classes' kites."

"That's dumb too!" Ronnie shouted in agitation. His gray eyes radiated the same level of disdain I had seen his father display when he bothered to accept my requests for meetings to discuss his son's behavior.

"Do you think Lightning McQueen thinks its dumb

when he gets on the racetrack?" I'd learned the hard way that the direct approach wouldn't work with Ronnie. Being the grandson of Jack Lawson IV, and a direct descendant of the town's founding family, made the kid nearly untouchable. That didn't mean I wouldn't keep trying to be the teacher I'd always wanted to be. Someone to nurture and open young minds to the possibilities of the world. Someone to help them find their potential—like a teacher had done for me. "McQueen's not trying to wreck the other cars, he's trying to push himself to do his best."

"I don't wanna be no loser." Ronnie crossed his arms. "I'm doing a dinosaur kite."

Great Mother, give me patience to deal with him today. Remember he doesn't have the best role models. His mom is scared of her shadow and his dad is a big bully. The kid is learning from his father's example.

I took a deep breath, hoping—maybe for once—I could get through to him.

"Win or lose, as long as you try your hardest you should always feel proud." I smiled at Ronnie, but he huffed and kicked his chair leg. "Does the class agree with Ronnie that we should make dinosaurs our theme?"

A hesitant little hand raised. "Yes, Amanda?"

"Uhm, maybe we can make butterflies?" Her big blue eyes darted to the side nervously checking on Ronnie sitting next to her. "We planted a butterfly garden at my house. My Mom is a hoot ... hort—uh, she grows plants. Mom says butterflies are important. They tell us when things are bad or good outside."

An image came to me. I was maybe seven and our apartment was so hot I was using damp washcloths to cool down. Mom hadn't been out of bed in days and the electricity had been turned off. Probably because she hadn't paid the bill

again. I had climbed out the window to the fire escape, too
restless to stay inside one minute longer. The steps had
made loud clanging noises as I climbed up to the rooftop.
Pots of flowers surrounded an area where someone had
placed a couple of rickety picnic tables. The flowers seemed
to call to me as I walked along touching their soft petals.
Dozens of yellow butterflies had come to land on the flowers. That afternoon had been the best in a while, as I spent
hours with the butterflies as my confidants, listening
intently.

Energy filled me. This was it.

"I love that idea!" I bounced excitedly as my artistic
juices started flowing with designs we could make. "What
do you say, class?"

There were a few grumbles, but almost everyone agreed.
I helped the kids to get their supplies together and walked
around to talk to them about their ideas. Then left them to
build whatever their imaginations came up with. I picked
up supplies for my own kite and sat down at my desk.
Creating art was almost like an out-of-body experience for
me. My hands worked diligently, while my vision turned
internally to focus on the image of what I wanted to create.
The designs came alive beneath my fingers as if by magic.

A shrill scream rang through the classroom jerking me
out of my daze. Agnes was under the table crying hysteri-
cally as she hugged her knees to her chest. Sheets of
construction paper, markers, and stickers littered the floor
around the middle table. Ronnie's table. He was concentrating really hard on gluing sticks to his paper at the
moment. That wasn't a good sign.

I gathered my long skirt and got down on my knees to
peek under the table. "Agnes, sweetheart, are you ok? What
happened?"

She sobbed harder. There was something gripped in her hand. I awkwardly leaned under the low table trying to get closer, but not scare her. I gently placed my hand on her arm and, when she didn't pull away, wrapped my arm around her shaking shoulders. "Are you hurt?"

"N-No. H-He ..." Agnes raised her head to look at me. The freckles across her cheeks stood out starkly against the paleness of her tear-streaked face. Over her right ear jagged stumps of hair stuck out in sharp contrast to the rest of her shoulder length copper curls.

"Oh no, honey, what happened to your hair?"

More tears slipped down her cheeks as she raised her hand to show me the large chunk of her hair. "R-Ronnie wanted my glue! I told him it was my turn."

My skin buzzed as anger filled me. It took everything I had not to shout at Ronnie and pull him out of that chair by his ear. I ran my fingers across the stubby ends of Agnes's hair, "I'm so sorry, sweetheart. Your hair is still beautiful; it'll just be a little different than normal. Hey, you can try out a new hairstyle, right? Different isn't always bad. What do you say we get out from under this table?"

She sniffled, "Is my mommy going to be mad at me?"

"No, sweetheart. She'll be upset, but not at you." Her mom would reserve all of her anger for me. This wasn't the first time I'd had to wipe away the tears and confront angry parents over something Ronnie had done. "But we need to go talk about this and call your parents. Can you come out now?"

She let me help her up but hid behind me as I sought out Ronnie. "Ronald Lawson, what on earth made you cut Agnes's hair?"

He squirted out a huge glob of glue, ignoring me. My

bangle bracelets rattled together as my irritation grew. "You can tell Principal Mathers all about it. Let's go."

Ronnie got up and shot a mean look at Agnes who was peeking around my hip. "Tattletale."

"That's enough, Ronnie. Let's go. Now." I turned to address the rest of the students. "Class, I want you to keep working on your kites. I'll be right back."

I took Agnes's hand and Ronnie trailed petulantly behind us as we left the room. I stopped to let Ms. Bresbane next door know what had happened and asked her to check on my class.

The administrative assistant gave me a sour look when we got to the front office. *Surprise! I'm back to file another complaint on the bully in my class. Let's hope this time Principal Mathers would actually do something.*

We were told to go in to the principal's office a few minutes later. Principal Edith Mathers sat behind her desk, her wrinkled lips pursed like she had bitten into a lemon.

"Ms. King, I hear there has been *another* incident with one of your classes. Is this the fourth time you've been in my office this year?" Perfectly arched eyebrows pulled down over her hard, hazel eyes. "Ah no, I believe this is the fifth. I try to forget that disaster with the ice."

I winced at the reference to the *Frozen* play we had put on right before spring break. Evidently ice melts really quickly when you apply the body heat of a dozen kids. The castle had been beautiful while it lasted, though.

"The ice was my fault. Those other visits were because of student concerns." My eyes drifted over to Ronnie. He stood there looking bored as he picked his nose. I turned away before I had to witness what he was going to do with the treasure he had just mined. "Which is why we're here again. Ronnie, why don't you tell Principal Mathers what you did?"

"I wanted to make a dinosaur kite. Ms. Dia said it was dumb." His lip poked out and his shoulders slumped. "She said we had to make butterfly kites. I ain't no girl."

That lying little ...

"Ronnie, that isn't what happened. Tell the truth," I gritted out. Heat rushed across my chest and up to my ears. I could swear steam was coming from them. "Tell her what you did to Agnes's hair."

He looked at his feet, mumbling, "Agnes put her head down on the table while I was cutting. I didn't mean to get her hair."

Agnes started crying again and buried her face against my waist. I smoothed my hand down her curls trying to soothe her as best I could in this awkward position.

"Principal Mathers, Ronnie's lying. He cut Agnes's hair because he wanted the glue she was using. He keeps bullying the other kids and it's getting worse. He—"

"Ms. King, that's enough." Principal Mathers pushed up her horn-rimmed glasses and steepled her fingers. "Did you see him cut Agnes's hair?"

"No," I said, "but Agnes told me what happened, and I believe her."

"I see." She pushed a button on her phone and barked out orders to her admin. "Call the nurse to take Agnes to her room to calm down. Call her mother in ten minutes and put her through to me. That will be all."

Principal Mathers turned to Ronnie. "I'm sure you feel horrible about this accident. It is generally Ms. King's decision on projects for her classes, but in this instance, I think we can make an exception. Art is about being creative after all. You have my permission to make your dinosaur kite. See Mrs. Mitchell for a hall pass and go straight back to your classroom. Thank you for being brave enough to tell me what happened."

Shock jolted through me. Agnes clutched me tighter when the admin entered and called her name. "You can't really—" I bit my tongue knowing that I was on the verge of saying something that would get me in trouble. The admin called for Agnes again, the poor girl refusing to let go of my leg. "At least, let me stay with Agnes and call her mom myself. As her teacher, I should be the one to explain this."

Agnes gripped me tighter before the admin grabbed her hand and pulled her away.

"Agnes, I hope you feel better soon," Principal Mathers said, ignoring me. "Ronnie go with Ms. Mitchell."

I felt a tug on my skirt as Ronnie shuffled by with his head still down and then they were gone.

"Ms. King have a seat." Principal Mathers ran a hand down her perfectly coiffed salt-and-pepper bob. Then straightened her already immaculate blazer with the school logo of a sailboat on it. I smoothed my skirt down to sit in the one of the chairs in front of her desk and my hand met a sticky substance. No, surely, he hadn't. I glanced down to find a slimy green booger smeared down the side of my skirt. I wanted to gag, but the principal was in full-on lecture mode.

"A teacher must always be in control of their classroom." Principal Mathers gave me a pointed look that said: "pay attention." "You seem to have some trouble in this regard. As the principal, when one of my teachers fails to do their job I am required to step in. That is what I am forced to do here today, since you appear to be too emotionally distraught to handle the situation."

"Principal Mathers, you can't really believe Ronnie over

Agnes. This isn't the first time he's done something like this."

"And you chose to believe Agnes over Ronnie." She pushed up her glasses, her eyes turning glacial. "You accused the son of one of our most prominent citizens of attacking another child without any form of proof. Did you ask any of the other children what happened?"

"No," I replied, thinking back over my actions. Had I jumped to conclusions? No. Agnes was quiet and sweet. She wouldn't blame him if it weren't true. "I probably should have asked them, and I can still do that. But I know he did this. Last week he pushed Dory because the finger paints she made looked better than his. The week before he locked Shelly in the supply closet when I was helping another student. His behavior is only going to get worse if he keeps getting away with this because of who his family is. His attitude, especially toward girls, is concerning."

"Ms. King, are you implying I wouldn't take action against a bully because his family funded this school and continues to make generous donations?" Her nose flared like she smelled something rotten. Her eyes pinned me in place with a glare of righteous indignation.

You are the only one standing up for those girls. Don't fail them now, Dia.

"I'm only saying that Ronnie needs the right guidance and I don't think he's getting that."

Principal Mathers's eyes narrowed, but after a moment she leaned back in her chair. "Ms. King, every student in our school is a lump of clay needing our hand to help mold them. Ronnie needs a bit more finesse than most. Being a teacher is a trying job. One not suited to everyone. You're a good teacher, but your ... eccentric ways prevent you from becoming an excellent one. I've made allowances, but no more. One more visit to my office and we will not be able to approve your tenure."

"B-But ... I've worked so hard. Surely—"

"This is your last chance, Ms. King," she said sternly. "You have come a long way from the young, impulsive girl you were as a substitute teacher. However, there is a certain image that we cultivate here at the W. C. Lawson Academy. One that I don't think you will ever fit. No more of these visits or I will be forced to let you go."

2

It was finally Friday and the day of our kite festival. The smell of fried food filled the air. Two rows of blue-and-white canopy tents lined one end of the school parking lot. I waved to a group of kids that were in line for the ring toss game. Then helped one of the volunteer parents refill cups of lemonade.

A couple of teachers stopped to congratulate me on pulling this all together. Happiness swelled inside me until I wanted to squeal. I was finally one of them. No longer was I the substitute teacher or "that new girl." I had brought the whole school together to enjoy this beautiful day and everyone was impressed. I was up for tenure in a few months and I couldn't wait. I would be one of the alumni and my career here would be set for life.

I ducked behind one of the game booths to check my phone again. My perfect future was within sight. All I needed now was for Dan to propose so we could start working on building our family together. Why hadn't he called yet? His flight should have landed hours ago.

Dan had been acting strange for months, but what

happened this morning had me really worried. I had been so excited, talking a mile a minute about the festival and bouncing around our bedroom. Dan had suddenly whirled on me and shouted at me to stop. I was so stunned by this completely out-of-character behavior that I backed right into the bed and sat on Mr. Skittles.

My cat had yowled like he was dying and squeezed his fluffy eight-pound body into the opening of Dan's duffle bag. If the noises that had come from that bag were any indication, the neat piles of clothes Dan had packed were not going to be usable for his conference. Instead of turning this into a lecture, he had simply smiled wistfully and said he would buy what he needed when he got to Reno. He had tugged on the Cinderella scrunchy that I used to keep my extremely long hair piled on top of my head and told me to never change. It was such a different Dan than I had grown used to these last five years, that he was out the door before I could even say goodbye.

My phone blasted "Can't Stop the Feeling!" from the *Trolls* movie as my alarm went off letting me know it was time to start the kite show. I glanced once more at my phone then made my way to the field where my students were getting ready for showtime. The music continued to play and lift my spirits. I stopped next to Amanda and shared a smile with her as I increased the volume on my phone. We were both big Poppy fans. She giggled as I started doing some of the dance moves from the movie. Kids joined me, and we were all laughing as we danced.

Principal Mathers stepped in front of me. Her lips puckered like they always seemed to be when I was around. She tapped the gold watch on her wrist. *What a slave driver. Wonder where she got that watch? Dance! Dance! Uh oh, the fun police are here! Oh right, gotta stick to the schedule.*

I turned off my phone. "Hi, Principal Mathers. We, uh, were just getting psyched up for the big show. Are you ready to be amazed?"

"Of course. You should go get ready." She gave the kids a thin-lipped smile. When the kids wandered back to their kites, she gave me a stern look. "Ms. King, you are behind schedule. This all needs to be cleaned up before dismissal."

"We're only a few minutes behind," I said. Yikes, someone should tell her the lip-pursing wasn't doing her wrinkles any favors. "Right, we're starting now."

I got the kids lined up and shouted, "Go!" They ran across the field and kites of all kinds took to the air. I stood next to the teacher panel of judges and cheered the kids on. There were so many great kites I would have given them all first place if I had been judging. A gust of wind sent the kites dipping and diving. Suddenly a dinosaur kite, bigger than the others by far, rammed into several other kites looking like it was eating them as they fell in mangled piles to the ground.

Ronnie! He weaved his way between the other kids leaving a trail of destroyed kites in his wake. Students started screaming and crying. I looked around for help, but the other teachers ducked their heads. Fine, guess I was the only one who would stand up to the little terror.

Principal Mathers watched with interest as I stomped across the field. No doubt waiting to see if I could handle this.

"Ronnie, stop!" I darted after him and managed to snag his kite string. He tugged back trying to get away, but I used it to reel him in. "We talked about this. Destroying the other kid's kites is mean. Look what you've done."

He looked over the scene of destruction with a satisfied

smile as more adults arrived to try to calm the other kids. "The Indominus was hungry."

Great Mother of the Earth! Never in my life had I wanted to spank a child until this moment. My fingers tightened around his kite string. Anger and frustration warred within me. *Your mother will disown you if you harm a hair on one living thing.* For someone of Romani heritage, banishment would be a death sentence for me. It didn't matter that we were only a tribe of two, family was everything.

I inhaled deeply taking in the scent of the grass and trees. As if Mother Earth felt my need for peace, an icy blanket calmed the mass of energy growing inside me. I let go of the kite string and stepped back.

Had the grass always been taller in this one section of the field? I dismissed the idea.

"You'll apologize to every kid right now. For the rest of the festival you will sit in the nurse's tent and write 'Being mean to others is bad' one hundred times. Do you understand?"

"This was a dumb party, anyway."

"Calling everything 'dumb' is being mean too," I admonished. "Now go say sorry."

The next couple of hours were spent handing out awards for the kite competition and packing everything up. My class and I were the only ones still around. Amanda proudly carried her first-place trophy as she helped pick up the remaining supplies from the craft booth. I handed another box to Ronnie, who had been released from his time out to help clean up. He stomped off toward the classroom with his load. I handed out more items to be carried back to class. Thankfully, we were going to have everything done with a little time to spare before dismissal.

I loaded my arms with the last of the boxes and headed

back to class. A strange noise caught my attention as I passed the large bronze statue of a sailboat at the front of the building. I stopped to listen, trying to identify what I was hearing. Was that squeaking noise coming from the statue? I walked around the other side where the plaque detailed how the Lawson family dedicated this statue to the school and was a replica of the first ship Jack Lawson IV had designed. Something dangled from the front of the boat. I rounded the side of the statue and the boxes in my hands fell to ground. Supplies spilled onto the asphalt. A gasp spilled from my lips.

Amanda was hanging from the bow of the ship like a giant spider had wrapped her up in kite string and left her there for a late-night snack. Tears glistened in her wide blue eyes. Her shrieks muffled by a band of tape. I lurched forward, my hands frantically searching for a way to get her down. Several of my other students had wandered back outside and were staring wide-eyed.

I carefully pulled the tape off Amanda's mouth, deciding I needed to know if she was hurt before getting her down.

"Amanda, sweetheart, are you ok?"

Her voice was choked off by sobs, but she nodded. Thank the Mother!

"Honey, don't move. We're going to get you down." I scooped up a pair of scissors that had fallen from the box and stuck them in my pocket. I pointed to a couple of boys. "You two, climb up on top of the statue and see if you can unhook the string from up there. I'll hold her, so she doesn't fall."

They found the string wrapped around a hook in the boat and worked together to get it untied. I gripped Amanda tightly. By then, the rest of my class had gathered around us.

The string went slack, and I set Amanda on her feet. "Hold still, honey. I'm gonna cut you loose."

I quickly cut the string away and Amanda threw herself into my arms. I hugged her close, thankful that she wasn't hurt. A scuffle sounded and the next thing I knew the boys who helped untie the string were pushing Ronnie toward me. His face was coated with rainbow streaks. He gripped the first-place trophy that Amanda had won for her kite in one hand. In the other was the stash of Skittles I kept in my locked desk drawer.

"He was hiding in the boat." One of the boys said, shoving Ronnie until he stumbled.

A surge of anger flashed through me until my world narrowed down to this one moment. To this one kid who terrorized so many others without consequence. But he had gone too far today. He had put another child's life at risk to steal her prize.

"Ronnie you're a bully. You hurt others for fun and attention just like your father. But you're both cowards." I scooped up a roll of pink duct tape. "Do you know what happens when the kids you bully finally realize that you don't have any power over them?"

"Huh?" He stared at me like I had lost my mind. He might have been right.

"They get even," I said as I handed the tape to Amanda. Then scooped up more rolls and gave them to the other kids.

I was admiring the kids' work when a supercharged engine purred and a sleek gray car pulled up in front of the school moments later. Principal Mathers stepped out of the school doors with the first smile I had ever seen from her. It slipped from her lips as she saw us gathered around the statue. "Ms. King, what are these students doing out here? Where's Ronnie, his father is here to pick him up?"

She rounded the statue and her face went white. Garbled sounds issued from her open mouth. The kids' laughter from only moments ago turned to worried looks, and they stepped away from their principal like she was a ticking bomb.

Ronnie was duct-taped to the side of the statue. His eyes the only part of him still visible under all of that pink tape. On the piece of tape across his mouth Amanda had placed the crowning touch. A neon orange sticker with a frog on it that said: *Improving by Leaps and Bounds.*

Principal Mathers's gaze darted uneasily to the idling car. "What is going on here, Ms. King?"

I turned to answer the principal.

"Justice."

3

I trudged numbly up the walkway to the house where I lived with Dan. The beige siding and brown trim of the one-and-a-half-storied bungalow was as conservative as the man who owned it. I stepped up onto the small front porch with the rock-accent columns and shifted the box in my arms to one side to unlock the door.

The familiar smell of cherry pipe tobacco and shoeshine greeted me like a soothing balm. I set the box down on the hall table and kicked off my shoes. If Dan were here, he would've been after me to put everything away in its proper place, like every other inch of this house. I tapped the corner of the picture of us that weekend I had forced him into a spontaneous trip to Colorado. The picture tilted to one side and I smiled, thinking of how he would pinch the bridge of his nose and his cheeks would get pink with irritation that one picture should dare not be straight.

There had been something about Daniel Walters that drew me from the first time I had seen him lecturing in his argyle sweater vest. I had been a college student assigned to be his teacher's aide. For a month, I had babbled like a brainless teenager every time he spoke to me. One misplaced lesson plan and seeing that cool composure slip had changed my life. I had become addicted to ruffling the feathers of the prudish history teacher.

We were perfect together. I kept him from being such a stick-in-the-mud and he kept me grounded when the noise in my head threatened to drown out the real world.

Mr. Skittle brushed up again my leg, drawing my attention and I bent to pet him. His face, legs, and tail all sported the darker brown colors typical of a ragdoll cat, while the rest of him was a lighter mixture of white and tan. His purring eased a little more of the ache over what had happened today.

Principal Mathers had lost her cool composure and started yelling at me. Which finally brought Ronnie's parents out of their car. His father had taken one look at his son and burst out laughing. Then suggested we leave him there, so he would learn to toughen up. His mother just stood there, wringing her hands. Anger had detonated in me like a grenade, shattering all of that peace I had worked toward. Ronnie's father had gotten an earful, and I had gotten fired on the spot.

Anger had carried me through packing up my desk, but the enormity of what I had done had sunk in on the drive home. Since my second-grade teacher had taken me under her wing, all I had ever wanted was to be like her. She had helped me to shake off the title of "that dirty gypsy girl" and find my confidence. If it wasn't for her my life would have turned out very different. When I became a teacher myself, I had kept my eye open for those kids that I could help in the same way she had helped me. I hadn't realized until it was too late that one of them was already right under my nose.

Ronnie had been acting out since he started school and

it had gotten worse over time. I had tried all kinds of approaches to correct his behavior, but nothing had worked. Instead of focusing on the behavior, I should have looked for the cause. Knowing his father was a bully, I should have dug deeper into what was happening at home. I should have realized how much Ronnie was like me at that age. The only difference was, I had turned inward to deal with my troubled home life instead of acting out.

I had failed Ronnie by letting my anger take over.

Regret and disappointment in myself settled like a heavy weight on my shoulders. I hugged my stomach, wishing there was someone to wrap me up in their arms and tell me it was going to be ok. Dan hadn't called. Lia was off playing house with her new boyfriend at her parent's house. At least, I thought she was. I hadn't really heard much from her lately. Not since she had recovered from the accident.

Lia had been injured in a boiler accident at her parents' house. Although, for some reason, I kept getting images of her flying through the air as wind whipped by and screams spilled from my mouth. It was strange. I know that isn't what had happened. I wasn't even there, but it seemed so real. I'd spent some time helping Lia as she recovered, and it had felt like old times again. Then she had moved into her parents' house and—nothing. Not that it mattered. Even when she or Dan were around lately, neither of them was fully here. I felt more alone than I had since I was a child.

My stomach rumbled, reminding me I hadn't eaten since lunch. Food was the last thing I wanted, but I knew myself well enough to know that an empty stomach would make me grumpy. I walked into the kitchen and grabbed a neatly labeled container of grilled chicken from Dan's side of the fridge and a cupcake, mostly covered in cling wrap, from my side. I sat the chicken on the island and pulled the cling wrap off the cupcake, licking the icing from it before tossing the wrap in the trash. A plain white envelope with my name on it caught my eye where it stood propped against the faucet of the sink.

"Awww, Dan left me a note."

My pink-icing streaked fingers left smudges on the envelope as I tore it open. A little bit of the gloom cleared away as I pulled out the first love note I had ever gotten from Dan. I hugged the paper to me for a moment, then started to read aloud:

Dia,

When we met, I was a sour old man still reeling from my wife divorcing me. Then you came into my life like a whirlwind of energy and color. You were so very young. Not just because of our age differences, but you still had dreams and ideas to make a difference in the world. I had long given up on my own. You showed me how to have fun again and I am grateful that I met you.

I should have told you this months ago, but I have never been good with the messier parts of life. When Melanie divorced me, I thought I would never find love again, but I was wrong. She and I ran into each other during that history lecture in Seattle. We started talking and realized how much we still loved each other.

There is no easy way to say this. I'm meeting her in Reno this weekend to get married again. She understood that you need a little time to move out of the house. We decided to take a long honeymoon and won't be back for a couple of weeks.

I hope you find someone who can give you the family you want. I'm not that person. I'm sorry.

Dan

My hands trembled as I read and re-read the letter. My knees felt like Jell-O, and I slid down to kneel on the floor. How could he do this? Five years we had been together, and he leaves me a note to break up? To tell me he's marrying his ex-wife again. That he's kicking me out of the house. My pulse pounded so loudly it felt like the floor was moving in time with the beat. Tears streamed like warm rain down my cheeks. Mr. Skittles pawed at my legs, and I could almost feel him asking what was wrong. I gathered him up and buried my face in his fur.

That perfect future I had been so close to achieving lay like the smoking remains of a burned-down bridge. Coldness seeped into my skin and sank down inside me to lock away the pain. The clamor in my head was silenced and all around me the world bled to gray.

The song "Every Day Is a Winding Road" filled the room as my cell phone vibrated in my pocket. A bitter laugh escaped me. I wanted to ignore it, but my mother would keep calling.

"Hi, Mama."

"*Chaj*, you have not called," she gently chided, calling

me "daughter" in the old Romani language, her accent still present, even after all these years in America. "I worry when you do not call for so many days. How is my baby?"

"It's only been three days since we talked." She made a disgruntled noise. "I know you worry, but I'm not a baby, Mama."

"You are always me baby," she said. "A mother is always a mother. Even when they do not act as one."

A cold sweat broke out as I was sucked into a memory from my childhood. A grief-stricken cry woke me in the night. The small, dark bedroom was suffocating. My nightgown was damp with sweat. I must have been four or five. My little legs barely able to reach the floor as I carefully avoided all the squeaky spots of the old mattress and got out of bed. I tiptoed to the cracked door and peeked out. A candle flickered on the battered coffee table in the small living room, the only light we had because Mama had forgotten to pay the electric bill again. Mama tossed and turned on the ripped and stained couch we had pulled from the curb. Her long hair was greasy and tangled. Her black dress sweat-stained. Even from here I could smell the sour stench. She cried and wailed in her sleep, begging someone not to leave.

"Claudia, are you there?"

I shook off the memories.

"Y-Yes Mama, I'm here. Please don't start apologizing again. You got help. You're better now. That's what counts." I gripped the phone until the case creaked. I couldn't talk about this today.

"What is wrong, my flower?" Her voice filled with alarm. "Do not deny. I hear in your voice the pain."

"I got fired and Dan left me to marry his ex," spilled from me in a tear-choked cry.

"I am sorry, my flower. I know your teaching mean much to you. But you will find other job. That man, he is *marime*." She declared Dan "unclean" in the Romani way of banishing people from the tribe. "He never good fit for you. You need passion and a man who love your spirit. Your heart hurts, I know. We will visit with the Great Mother together, yes?"

"You're right. A visit to the woods would calm me," I said as I wiped my tears away.

"You are close to the Great Mother. Even as a child you talked to her and the flowers before you talked to people." One of those laughs I cherished so much because they had been missing for so long floated over the phone line, and I was suddenly really glad my mother was coming over. "Remember to always worship the Great Mother and she will help you when you need her. Now, I come get you."

4

The bell over the door tinkled as another customer entered Whimsy Fine Arts. It had taken some time to find a job in our small town. Luckily, Ms. Myrtle had needed the help since she was now the proud owner of this art gallery. With Lia's move back to Mercer Island, she hadn't wanted the long commute here and had sold the gallery to Jack Lawson IV. He had given it to his wife, Ms. Myrtle, when they had married a couple of weeks ago.

Business seemed to be picking up now that all the fake rumors about Lia had died down. Of course, Ms. Myrtle being the leader of the town busybodies wouldn't have put up with any rumors damaging her new business, anyway. She may have been in her fifties, but she could twist an ear like nobody's business. Not to mention that she was now married to the most influential man in town. When she hired me as her assistant, she had only asked that, if I felt like taping anyone up, I give her a little warning so that she could charge for admission. It had been a little weird since she was now Ronnie's father's new stepmother, but when I asked if hiring me would cause her trouble, she said her husband had laughed his cute butt off when she told him her plans. That lady scared me, but we worked well together.

The art classes she was letting me set up was a great example of this. Ms. Myrtle had liked my idea of offering art classes on the weekends. The idea had come from my need for extra cash and to alleviate the boredom of selling art rather than creating it. I missed working with kids and having the freedom to create. My hopes were high for this first class. A small crowd had gathered around the area where I had arranged a U-shaped section of tables. Drop cloths covered the floor. Easels with blank canvases sat on the tables along with brushes and paper plates.

A group of children were gathered around the cat carrier that sat on the ledge of the fireplace where Mr. Skittles was finishing his nap. He had been a bit grumpy since we had moved into Lia's condo and was no longer allowed to roam wherever he wanted. I kept telling him we would find our own place any day now, but I could tell not even he was convinced by my lies. The truth was there wasn't enough money left over every month to afford the payments on the few rentals that were available in town. Lia had refused to take any of my money, but it felt wrong. These classes had to be a success.

Missy, an English teacher I had once joked about lesson plans with, broke up an argument between her two middle girls. Her oldest daughter, a teen with her face glued to her cell phone, nodded absently at whatever her mother was saying. While Missy was distracted, the youngest toddled straight for a shelf of blown-glass animals. I rushed forward to scoop her up just before her sticky fingers landed on all of that colorful glass.

"Birdy! Want birdy!" the squirming little girl squealed, reaching toward the cabinet.

"Look, we're flying. Let's fly to mommy," I coaxed.

We zoomed around making airplane noises. The little girl giggled, successfully distracted from the breakables as I flew her into her mother's arms. Missy thanked me with a weary smile. Her wiry brown hair was a frizzy mess and she only had eye liner around one eye. I patted her arm in sympathy, and decided I was going to find a way to keep those girls' attention no matter what. My own problems were on the back burner at least for the next hour. I was going to prove to everyone, including myself, that I still knew how to have fun.

"Hi, everyone! Thanks for joining Mr. Skittles and me today. I'm so glad you saw my flyers and decided to give 'Painting with Kitty Picasso' a try! If you could take a seat, we'll get started."

"Like anyone could've missed your flyers. It looks like a rainbow threw up all over town." A black-haired boy who looked to be about eight rolled his eyes as he dropped into a chair. His mother elbowed him. He flopped back in his seat and crossed his arms. "What? You said I had to come to this lame painting thing as my punishment. I'm missing gaming with Ty to listen to the crazy gypsy lady talk about her cat. This blows."

The mother blushed and whispered furiously to her son.

I smiled brighter and fanned out my green tie-dyed skirt as I dropped into a curtsy.

"You've found me out, sir. We prefer the name Romani rather than gypsy, though." I glanced at the boy to see I had caught his attention. "Did you know that a long time ago my people weren't welcome in parts of Europe? They had to move around a lot to stay safe. Most never had a country, a religion, or a home like we do. But do you know what all Romani do have?"

The boy was frowning now, but he shook his head.

"Love of family," I said proudly. "Just like you, coming here with your mother. That was a very nice thing for you to do."

The boy grumbled, but he watched his mom out of the corner of his eye. She patted him on the shoulder and a small smile tugged at his lips. *Ah ha, not such a tough egg after all.*

"Did you know that some Romani never attend school? Everything they learn comes from their large family groups. Things like nature, music, art, and dance." My arms lifted in a complicated series of twists as my slippered feet tapped out a quick beat. Then my skirt flared as I twirled around and dipped into a low spin. It had been years since I had practiced, but some things you never forgot. "My people gave us the Flamenco dance."

My audience applauded. I straightened up looking at the boy to see his reaction. He was sitting forward in his seat a look of awe on his face. "They don't have to go to school? Mom, I wanna be a gypsy."

His mother shot me a dirty look.

Uh oh, my first attempt at entertainment and I accidentally start anarchy. This isn't off to a great start.

"Um, time to paint!" I called out cheerfully. "You all have your canvases in front of you. I'm going to come around and put some paint on your paper plates. This is water-based paint, so it's non-toxic for Mr. Skittles and for all of you."

Making my way around the room, I handed out smocks and helped them get their palettes ready. Then I moved to the cat carrier. "Now, the moment you've all been waiting for. Let's bring out our artist."

Gently, I pulled the languid ball of fur from the carrier. Mr. Skittles opened one bright blue eye and yawned. I sat him on the table beside his canvas as the kids squealed in delight. Realizing that he had an audience, he lazily flopped onto his back waiting for the petting to begin. His purr vibrated against my hands as I picked him up and walked him around so the kids could stroke his soft fur.

Mr. Skittles puffed out his chest when I set him back on the table. I could practically feel how pleased he was to be the center of attention. I nudged the palette toward him and placed his paw in the blue paint. Unfortunately, the first thing he did was try to lick the paint off. "Mr. Skittles, don't eat that!" I scooped him up and turned in time to see half of the kids trying to do the same thing. "Um, let's maybe not follow exactly what Mr. Skittles does."

The boy from earlier snorted. "She doesn't know what she's doing."

"Mr. Skittles is feeling a little shy," I hastily explained while wiping his paw. "Maybe you can give him some encouragement?"

"Kitty, paint!" yelled Missy's youngest. "Kitty, paint, paint!"

Others joined in clapping and shouting for Mr. Skittles. I rubbed his head silently pleading with him to be feeling artistic today. The pressure was on. After all, this was a little different than when he puked up a rainbow on T-shirts after sneaking into my stash of Skittles. Like any artist, he could be really moody about his art. I'd learned the hard way, after he left a surprise in my shoe, not to push him when he wasn't into creating.

Come on, buddy, time to make the kids happy. We need these classes.

Suddenly something brushed up against my mind like the smooth, flexible surface of a balloon. The presence vibrated in tune with the purring beneath my palm. What in the name of the Mother was happening? Sure, my head was busy with noises and voices, but I'd never felt this before. It had been so quiet lately in my mind that I jumped when the sensation came again and random thoughts flooded in. *Fishes. Nice lady. Pet more. Sticky paw. Water. Fishes swim. Nice lady.*

I jerked my hand away from Mr. Skittles and the voice stopped. Surely that couldn't be—? I had always had an affinity with animals, but that was mostly a general sense of how they were feeling. Had I been able to hear an animal's thoughts all along but never noticed because my mind had never been this quiet? I put my hand on his head again. *Nice lady. Pet more.* He bumped my hand with his head. *Good. Pet. Feed soon.* His rough tongue licked my finger. Oh wow, this was amazing. I pushed the palette toward him again careful to keep my other hand on his head. *Sticky paw. Water. Fishes swim.*

One of the parents cleared their throat and asked if I was ok. I beamed at my restless audience thrilled with my new discovery. "Mr. Skittles has decided we should draw fish swimming in the water. Let's start with the blue paint."

5

Today was my day off. It should have been easy enough to relax—I at least had a job now. But a weird dream had woken me up in the early hours of the morning. All I could remember was blue eyes and darkness. I'd felt unsettled ever since. The other news I'd heard yesterday hadn't helped either. I kneeled on the floor of Lia's condo having a staring contest with Mr. Skittles. He batted my nose with his paw, and I blinked.

"Hey, no cheating."

He meowed. Then dislodged my hand as he turned in a circle before flopping down on the couch. I propped my chin on the edge of the gray leather cushion and sighed. We had been at this off and on all day. Why couldn't I hear his thoughts now?

The class yesterday hadn't gone like I had pictured. The painting had just started to come together when a brown-and-white basset hound had barreled through the door. He knocked over the customer coming in and headed straight for Mr. Skittles. My cat had nearly jumped out of his skin trying to run away, but his paint-covered paws slowed him down.

Mr. Skittles jumped on me as if looking for a savior and wrapped himself around my head. I couldn't see a thing as the dog barked and ran circles around me. My skirts had become tangled up with his leash and we had gone crashing into the table. It gave an ominous creak before collapsing, sending supplies flying everywhere. Paint splattered the whole area, including my class. Kids cried. Adults shouted. The dog's owner had finally untangled us, calling out apologies as he dragged his pet toward the door. But the gallery and my class were ruined.

After Ms. Myrtle had wiped away her tears of laughter and bandaged the claw marks on my forehead, she had declared that the classes weren't going to work. Wearily, I'd dragged myself and my paint-covered cat back to the condo. Hours of scrubbing later, I'd dropped into exhausted sleep. Only to be woken up by a text from Lia telling me she was coming for a visit. It had been a long time before I was able to get back to sleep.

A chill skated down my arms, and I rubbed them trying to stay warm. The thermostat was cranked up to eighty degrees. I was dressed in a soft pair of knit leggings and a long-sleeved sweater, but still couldn't get warm. Maybe I was sick. Maybe I had a fever that was making me imagine hearing Mr. Skittles' voice yesterday. Never mind that I had taken my temperature a dozen times.

"What are you thinking, boy?" I asked for the millionth time.

Mr. Skittles rolled onto his back purring and twisting about until he could rub his head against my cheek. "If this is your way of apologizing for scratching me ... it's working." I rubbed his belly until he yawned and curled up for a nap.

Sinking back onto my butt, I pulled my knees to my chest. My toes wiggled into the plush cream carpet as I wondered what to do next. I'd killed time by turning a couple of old shirts into scarves and painting flowers on a pair of jeans. I couldn't avoid thinking about it forever, but I needed at least today.

I'd woken feeling like I had barely slept and forced myself to go to yoga class. After we were done, I had felt more centered and found the courage to ask my instructor if I could teach a couple of classes. Her eyes were as big and round as saucers as she hastily assured me that she didn't have anything available. I had thanked her and crossed yoga classes off my list as another source of income. Only later in the locker room, I had overheard her telling another student she was terrified that I would turn her class into a circus like what had happened at the gallery. I'd gotten the same response from my self-defense instructor, although he had at least told me to my face that my ability to cause pandemonium wasn't a good fit for people trying *not* to injure each other.

I rubbed my eyes and pushed to my feet. My usual energy was nonexistent, and it would be too easy to sleep the rest of the day away. I walked to the large bay window at the back of the condo's living room. Ocean waves crashed against the grassy green shoreline. Seagulls dipped with the breeze and, for a moment, I wished I could be as free. I shook my head and tried to dislodge the dreary thoughts. This wasn't like me. I had determined long ago that I would make my own happiness no matter what, but I had been struggling to keep that promise to myself lately.

A knock at the front door interrupted my thoughts. I walked across the living room and past the kitchen to open the door.

"Sorry I'm late." Lia gripped me in a hug as soon as the door swung open. The air rippled in that weird way it had been doing whenever she was around lately. "It seems like it's been ages since I saw you." She stepped back to look me over. "Why do you look like Eeyore? The woman who glued glitter thongs on Dan's pants after he dumped you and told off a rich bully should not be looking like the sky is falling."

I was barely able to close the door as she grabbed my hand and hauled me to the couch.

"Eeyore is cute," I said as I tried to smooth down my hair. "He just needs a hug,"

Had I combed my hair today? Oh, well, it was only Lia.

"Is that what you need, a hug?" She eyed me with a look of pity that made me feel like a failure. Not that I needed her confirmation, when I already felt that way. "You've lost weight, and you're wearing all gray, for fuck's sake. I didn't know you even owned neutral colors."

"I'm trying something new."

"Uh huh. Why is it so hot in here?" She fanned herself, then crossed to adjust the thermostat. "You shouldn't try hot yoga by yourself. I'm about ready to pass out from the heat, and I've only been here a minute."

She was allergic to all forms of exercise, so it made sense.

"Is *hiding* something new you're trying too?" Lia continued. "Take it from someone who knows: it doesn't help." She dropped onto the couch, still fanning herself. "You had to have heard that Ronnie and his mom moved out. I thought you would feel better about the whole school incident after that."

"Yeah, his mom stopped by the gallery. She thanked me for standing up to her husband. And said what I did gave her the courage to leave him. Ronnie apologized to me, too."

It still amazed me the good that had come from that day. I still missed teaching like crazy, but the guilt over not helping Ronnie had lessened.

"If it's not that, you must have heard the other news going around town." Lia shifted on the couch to wrap her arm around me. "I'm sorry, Dia. I know how much you wanted a family."

I flinched as she managed to rip open the wound I had been trying so hard to avoid acknowledging. I had cried for an hour in the gallery bathroom after a customer had told me that Dan and his new wife were expecting. For some reason, that had felt more like a betrayal than the Dear John letter. Dan had refused to talk about starting a family when we were together. I thought it was because he didn't want kids, but he just hadn't wanted them with me.

I ducked my head and tugged at a loose thread in the hem of my sweater. Tears stung the backs of my eyes, but I fought hard not to let them fall. I knew Lia meant well, but right now it felt like she had shown up out of the blue only to rehash everything that was wrong with my life. When I had composed myself enough to look at her without crying, she had a glazed look on her face. The one she got often the few times we had hung out over the last couple of months. She would suddenly go quiet and emotions would flicker across her face like she was having a conversation with someone only she could hear. I wanted so badly to ask, but the habit of letting Lia open up in her own time was hard to break.

I knew she was making changes to her life and trying harder to let others in. But she was still holding back. The abruptly halted conversations and secret looks were enough to tell me that. Lia always wanted to protect me, no matter how often I'd told her not to put me in a bubble. Deep down, I knew that it wasn't because she didn't trust me, but it hurt just the same. She had Bennett now, and I couldn't help but wonder where that left me.

She rubbed her temples and gave me an apologetic little smile. "I'm sorry. I thought we would have more time. Bennett made me late." She blushed. "Well, anyway, company's coming."

6

"Lia, no. You know what happened last time we met." I stared at her incredulously after she told me who was coming.

"Oh yeah, this should be interesting," she chuckled. A groan escaped me, and she raised her hands in defense. "Hey, it was his idea. I want it on record that I am not in agreement with his plan. I'm here to have your back and referee if he needs protecting."

"What if *I* need protecting?"

"I think you can handle him." She gave me a knowing look. "But if I see you starting to fall under his charm, I'll protect your virtue."

Heat swept across my chest and I jumped to my feet frantically scanning the condo. I rushed into the kitchen, and Lia followed me, laughing. I gathered all of the dishes scattered across the kitchen counters and dumped them haphazardly in the dishwasher. I wiped down the splatters from the pot of spaghetti warming on the stove. Then tucked the basket of avocados I'd taped silly faces onto into a cabinet. The bag of Skittles went into the flour canister.

The clay pots of veggies that looked like flower arrangements went into the freezer.

I rushed back into the living room to scoop up a pair of socks and stuffed them under a couch cushion. Choking sounded, and Lia stumbled from the kitchen. Pieces of the spaghetti I had made were plastered to the front of her shirt looking like fat worms with their rusted reddish-brown color. Her eyes were wide. Her face bright red as she shoved pieces of ice into her mouth while trying to talk. It sounded like she said, "Dahea da goo gee hee."

"Are you ok?" I went over to pat her on the back. She said something else unintelligible. "No matter how many times you try, I'm never going to speak Ewok."

"You shouldn't mock Ewokese," she rasped out. "Oh gods, what did you put in that? My throat feels like I swallowed a hot coal. I didn't think it was possible to mess up spaghetti."

"Uh, cayenne?" I winced as she crunched more ice. The jar of cayenne had only been about one-third full, but maybe dumping the whole thing in hadn't been such a great idea. My mom had never used a measuring cup. She always said you would know the right mixture when you felt it in your bones. Cooking was supposed to be an art. Apparently, my bones were picky about what they considered art. I could put together a color palette blindfolded, but cooking was beyond me. Give me salad with a Skittles chaser any day.

The doorbell rang. Holy pink paint drops, I wasn't ready for this!

Ohhh, sexy is in the house! No, he's outside. Don't trust him. You had a bad breakup recently, how can you be lusting after this man already? Lust is most likely to occur when the person does not resemble themselves.

STOP!

The chatter in my brain faded away and I took a relieved breath. What was wrong with me? Sometimes the voices in my head were so overwhelming that I couldn't take it. Maybe my mother wasn't the only one who needed help.

I ran my hand over my loose hair and my eyes went wide. *I hadn't brushed my hair.* Lia laughed at my panic. I threw a dish towel at her and went to get the door.

Mister hotshot lawyer stood on the small front stoop looking sexier than any man had a right to in well-worn jeans and a sky-blue T-shirt. His shoulder-length dishwater blonde hair was windblown, like he had been driving with the windows down. Those midnight-blue eyes scanned me from head to toe and that irritating smirk kicked up one corner of his full lips. The chill from earlier disappeared like it had never been. A warm breeze caressed my bare shoulder where my sweater had slipped.

"You don't have any picket signs laying around, do you?" Jaxon Baines flashed a smile guaranteed to slay any woman.

Butterflies took flight in my stomach. *He'll probably invite you to his bed again. Yes, please! No, you aren't interested, remember. Look at those lips. No, his chest is his best feature.*

SHUT UP! Why did my head have to pick now to get noisy again?

"I've retired from picketing." I crossed my arms. "The hours were lousy, and I got propositioned by strange men."

"They must have good taste." He stepped into the doorway, his body brushing against mine before I could step out of the way. That warm breeze fluttered over my neck and then traced down between my small breasts. I shivered with desire. He tugged at a lock of my hair. "I miss the feathers, but this suits you."

He ran his finger around the messy little flower design I

had twisted the chunk of hair into, and I jumped, feeling that touch circle my belly button. Jaxon wound my hair around his finger, reeling me in to him. My breath caught as those midnight eyes settled on my lips, and they tingled, remembering the brief kiss we had shared right before he left town.

I had relentlessly hounded him when he had been in Port Lawson to get Lia out of jail. I had slapped glittery stickers like warning labels on those muscular arms telling myself someone had to warn the helpless ladies of our town about the hot lawyer who flirted like it was an occupation. My colorful classroom stickers had been altered to say things like: *I Put My Hand Up ...Women's Skirts.* Besides I needed to make sure that boring suit and beautiful face weren't all bluff. He was there to do a job, and I was going to make sure Lia was in good hands.

Jaxon had been amused at first, but when he realized I wasn't going away, he had tried to ditch me. He hadn't stood a chance. To be fair, he didn't know that I'd learned every corner of this town as a child when hiding from bullies who thought a lonely gypsy girl was an easy target. He'd confronted me on his last day in town, and we'd had a heated argument. I had been mid-lecture about privileged lawyers who thought they were better than the little people when he had pressed his lips to mine and obliterated every thought in my head.

"Virtue alarm! Virtue alarm!" Lia called out in a robot-voice, jerking us out of whatever that had been.

Jaxon looked confused for a moment before that grin came back. "What can I say, she thinks I'm irresistible."

I pulled my hair out of his grasp and stepped back. "I don't think of you at all."

He went to the chair across from the couch and flopped

down. "No really, she followed me around town like a lost little puppy looking for attention when I was here a few months ago."

"I ... You ... No, I didn't." I closed the door harder than necessary and stomped over to the couch.

"As entertaining as this is, can you hurry this up, Jaxon? Grayson is going to track me down in about ten minutes." Lia looked out the front window as if her new personal assistant would pop up at any minute. "Ever since he moved into my parent's house with me, I swear he thinks he needs to be glued to my side. I've had to get really creative about ditching him. Just say 'no,' Dia, and I'll let you torture me with shopping. That should keep him busy."

"No to what?" I asked.

"Dia, we have a problem that I think you can help us with." Jaxon ignored Lia and sat forward in the chair, his elbows braced on his wide-spread knees. The serious look on his face took me by surprise. "Do you remember the games that Lia went to? They're very important to the company I work for. The company that runs the Games. The thing is, all six of the Games have to be completed within every calendar year. There are some very boring contracts involved, but the point is the company is in jeopardy if they don't fulfill the obligation."

Lia snorted something that sounded like "Bullshit."

"What does this have to do with me?" I asked.

Jaxon pulled a card from his back pocket and set it down on the coffee table. The index-sized card looked familiar.

"Isn't that the invitation to the games? But it had writing on it before?"

"The writing only appears when the right person touches the card," Jaxon replied. "Why don't you pick it up?"

Curiosity filled me. I know I had seen writing on this

card before. Did he mean I was one of the "right" people? I picked up the plain card and, for a second, nothing happened. Then it felt like something bit my finger. Before I could jerk my hand away, a tiny drop of blood beaded on the edge of the card then sank into the paper. The world seemed to expand around me, and it was like I was looking down on myself. I had a moment to take in how pale and bedraggled I looked before I slammed back into my body. I opened my mouth to ask what for the love of pink just happened when writing began to curl onto the page like vines growing up through a crack. Had this happened before when I touched the card? It seemed vaguely familiar.

YOU ARE CHOSEN.
CHILD OF SPIRIT.
WHAT YOU SEEK YOU COULD FIND.
FAMILY. DESIRE. PURPOSE.
ALL COULD BE YOURS IN THE PALDIMORI GAMES.
SPIRIT OF THE SOUL
ANERRHIPHTHO KYBOS

"Shit," Lia said with a huff.

I dropped the card and scrambled to my feet. "What was that?"

"That," Jaxon said with a satisfied smile, "is your invitation to join the Games. If you come to the island and finish out the remainder of the Games, the company will guarantee you a teaching position in any of the schools that we support. As extra incentive, we will double your previous salary."

"You need to think about this. The Games can be dangerous." Lia sat on the coffee table and took my hands in hers. "Things are different on the island. People don't play by the same rules. There is—"

"Lia, you can't—" Jaxon cut her off.

"Shush, Cupid, before you find out what it feels like to get shot by your own arrow." Lia glared at him meaningfully. There was some kind of power struggle going on with that stare. Jaxon fisted his hands, anger flashing in those dark eyes, as he slouched back into the chair.

The look on Lia's face had all of my attention.

"I'm not kidding, Dia. The Games are more than challenging, they can be really dangerous. I couldn't stand it if you got hurt."

"You would be my contestant," Jaxon interjected, his calm composure back in place. "You have my promise that I'll keep you safe, Dia."

I scowled at them both. "I keep telling all of you, I don't want to be put in a bubble, but you never listen. For the last time, I can take care of myself."

"Dia—" Lia gave me that same pitying look, like I was too naive to realize what I was getting into.

Stung to the core, I pulled my hands from hers. "This is my decision, not yours. All I've ever wanted is to be a teacher. I've been trying to accept that that part of my life was over, but it's killing me. If I have a chance to get that back, I'm taking it."

"I'm sorry," Lia whispered. "I know it's your choice. I only want what's best for you. I can't compete in the Games since they voided my contract, but I'm not letting you go alone."

My irritation faded away and I hugged her. "I know." I turned to Jaxon. "I'm in," I said.

Jaxon clapped his hands. "Welcome to the Paldimori Games, Claudia King."

7

The plane dived toward the coastline of the island below. My nose was pressed to the window, a smile plastered across my face. Captain Jack was a fun pilot. He banked sharply to the left, startling a giggle out of me as my belly dipped. Then we were doing a roll, and I threw my hands up in the air laughing. This was even better than a rollercoaster! Across the aisle, Molly cussed as she tried to hold onto her laptop while hanging upside down. Her short white-blonde hair with the blue-tipped ends floated around her head for a moment making her look like an angry porcupine.

The plane completed the roll, the seatbelt releasing me from its tight grip as gravity plopped me back into my seat. My breath fogged the window and I drew a heart over the view of the island below. Everywhere I looked was paradise. A waterfall fell over a rocky cliff into an aqua-blue lagoon. There was a field bursting with flowers in every color imaginable. A pod of dolphins raced around rocks that jutted toward the sky in amazing formations off the coast of a sandy white beach.

The shade of the window slammed down barely missing my nose.

Molly sank back into her seat with a grumbled, "Keep it closed."

It was really hard to believe this was the same woman Lia had told me about while helping me pack. I had expected fun and mischievousness, not cold disdain. Molly had barely said a word since picking me up earlier. I had been so relieved to see Captain Jack's friendly face waiting at the top of the steps to the plane that I'd hugged him without thinking. Molly had roughly bumped into me as she passed by, and it was then I remembered Lia mentioning that the woman may have had a little crush on the handsome pilot. Captain Jack had angrily told her to watch what she was doing. Molly had whirled around, eyes blazing, and I was sure she was going to blast us both. But she had just walked away.

I was pulled from my thoughts when the plane touched down with a jostling lurch. I almost asked if I could open the window, but figured it wasn't worth the arctic blast from Molly. The plane rolled to a stop a few minutes later and we got up to grab our bags. I stopped by the cockpit to joke with Captain Jack about his flying. The lighthearted conversation welcome after all I'd been through lately.

"Keep it in your pants until later. You're messing with my schedule," Molly glared at us, then exited the plane.

My shocked gaze met the captain's irritated one. "Is she always like that?"

"No. Well, no to most people. Molly's been through a lot lately, but she's so damn stubborn," he sighed. "She's mad at the world right now and taking it out on everyone. It didn't help that she heard Lia was coming back. I mean—"

"I thought they were friends? That's what Lia said."

"They were ... are ... it's complicated." He brushed a hand nervously through his hair. "Look, Molly'll deal with this and be back to kicking life in the balls soon enough. I've known her since she was a teenager. She's bossy and rude on the best of days. And can be a violent little thing." He absentmindedly rubbed at his stomach as if remembering some abuse at her hands. "But you can trust her. As your guide, she'll protect you with her life. But I'm willing to bet you'll win her over soon enough. She would do anything for those she considers a friend. Give it some time."

I could sympathize, but I wasn't sure there was a lumberjack up to the task of whittling away that chip on her shoulder. I hoped things got better for her, but I couldn't let her problems ruin my best chance at getting what I wanted. It was time to put me first for a change.

"You're probably right. Thanks, Jack, for being here to help ease me into this. I had hoped Lia would be here, but she had a change of plans." I tried to keep the disappointment from my voice and forced a smile. "It was nice to see a friendly face. I hope I'll see you around."

Those dimples came back out full force. "Count on it. Good luck in the Games."

I shouldered my bag and made my way down the steps of the plane. Cool air and the smells of fuel, grease, dampness, and a hint of floral greeted me. We were in an honest to goodness cave! My head swiveled left and right trying to take it all in. Which is probably why I found myself airborne a moment later. My knees hit the rock floor with a heavy thud that radiated up to my hips causing me to grunt in pain. Luckily, I got my hands in front of me before my face smacked into the ground. The rough rock shredded my palms.

Steps one, me zero. We had a long-standing feud.

Before I could pull myself up, alarmed voices echoed through the cave. Then there was a sound like rushing wind. Molly shouted something, but I couldn't make it out. I tried to crawl back to the safety of the plane, but I couldn't move. My hands were sinking into the rock like it was putty.

Amazing, two seconds on this island and I land in quicksand. This is not a good sign for how the Games are going to go.

Breath whooshed out of me as I frantically tried to pull my hands out. Then something tickled along my cheek. Then my nose. My neck. My arms. Something tangled in my hair and settled along my back.

I held absolutely still. My breaths sawed out, shallow and fast. A cold sweat popped up along my brow. I really, really hoped that whatever was crawling all over me didn't have teeth or any kind of stinger. My wide-eyed gaze found Molly's. There was this indescribable expression on her face like a cross between devastation and grim determination. Her eyes were brimming with tears. Her fists clenched at her sides as she took sliding steps to reach me.

Great Mother, was it that bad?

The fluttering sensations covered my whole body, but other than the throbbing in my hands from where I had fallen, there was no pain. I forced myself to take deep breaths. Then finally I looked down at my arms. I'd expected to find my skin crawling with ugly cave creatures, but what I saw had my mouth dropping open in awe. Then I snapped it closed just as quickly to avoid having anything crawl inside.

I was covered in dozens of bright yellow butterflies. The rushing wind sound undulated like waves around us. I looked up to see millions more butterflies weaving some complicated pattern above me. They made one final swoop, and I swear I saw the distinct pattern of a woman waving at me from their midst.

Just as quickly as they came, they were gone. The silence left in their wake seemed almost reverent. I sat back on my knees and rubbed my tingling arms.

I'm free! Thank you, Mother Earth, Santa Claus, and the Easter Bunny!

I got to my feet only to find I was the center of attention. Even Captain Jack was staring at me as if I were some truly amazing, but bizarre, circus act. I wrapped my arms around myself. Their stares brought back too many memories from my childhood and all of those eyes condemning me because I was different.

"Ok, people, show's over." Molly shouted, making me jump. "Are you deaf? Leave, or I'm sending you all to clean Eros's rooms. And no one will come looking for you."

People scattered quickly after that. Whoever Eros was he must have been a real slob.

"Dia, are you ok?" Molly walked hesitantly toward me as if afraid I would run off if she made any sudden movements.

I carefully got to my feet, avoiding putting weight on my stinging palms. "I'm fine. Just skinned up a bit. Um, do you welcome everyone with their own personal butterfly show?"

"No," Molly gritted out. Her face was pale, and her fists were still clenched. Was she going to hit me? "That's never happened before."

"That was amazing." I took a tentative step back. "A little icky with the crawling all over me part, but they're beautiful."

"Yes, they are." Molly cocked her head to the side and looked me over. "Where's your family from?"

That was an odd question to ask. "Washington."

"Not you." Molly huffed as the fingers of her left hand

tapped rhythmically over her thigh. "Your great-grands. Your ancestors."

"Well, my family is Romani. Most people call us—"

"Gypsies. Yeah, I'm familiar. What else?"

The captain had been right about the rude and bossy parts. I just hoped that I could avoid her violent side. I was fairly sure Molly could shred me like compost even with my self-defense training.

"My mom has never been big on talking about her family." She would tell me stories about growing up in the tribe. It'd sounded so amazing to be surrounded by so much love and understanding. No matter how much I'd begged, though, she would never tell me where they were or why she'd left. "All I know is that my father abandoned us before I was born. My mom left her tribe soon after and raised me on my own."

"Hmm. You ever have that happen before?"

She shifted more gears than my bicycle. "What?"

"The butterflies. Anything like that happen to you before?"

"No, I can honestly say I don't go around with an escort of butterflies. That would be kinda cool though, right? But maybe with cats. Mr. Skittles could be the leader of the kitty parade. He would look super cute with a top hat and sash that said: *Grand Marshal of Kitty Entourage*. Of course, it would have to be pink. It's his favorite color. Too bad he had to stay with Ms. Myrtle. He would—"

The sound of a camera shutter clicking rapidly cut into my rambling. Molly was completely ignoring me to take pictures of the ground. Right. Well, guess she was all out of weird questions.

"Let me see your hands." Or not.

"Say what now?"

"Hands. Let me see 'em." Molly had moved closer and held her phone at the ready. "Palms up."

With both scrapped and bloody palms held out in front of me, she started snapping pictures. The injuries seemed to form some kind of shape. It almost looked like ... No, it couldn't be. My artist's eye had to be making more of the lines than was really there.

Molly must have noticed my quizzical expression. "The ground is the same. They look like ..."

"Lotus flowers," we said at the same time.

8

Dinner had been a rushed affair since I was the last to arrive and the only newbie in the group. Devon, the hulking leader of the guides, had introduced me as Lia's friend in that gravelly voice of his and it hadn't sounded like he considered that a good thing. Then the contestants had introduced themselves like a lightning round of speed dating. Luckily, being a teacher, I'd learned to pick up names quickly. There was Kade, the guy who wore a cowboy hat and had the cute Southern twang. I had to stifle my chuckle when I remembered Lia had called him "Cowboy Cutie." She was always good for a funny nickname for people.

Chris, the youngest of the bunch, reminded me of a better-looking Shaggy from *Scooby-Doo*, all gangly and completely out of his element. Mikhail, a lean man with dark black skin, glared at everyone suspiciously. Maya was a tall Asian woman who wore a very boring gray pants suit and whipped out a calculator as soon as we were introduced. And Nikki, who was all blonde, bubbly, and had a curvy shape that I envied. I almost choked on my wine when I remembered Lia had called her "Busty Bigmouth." It was so appropriate.

I made a mental note about all the contestants, realizing that I was going to be in for a challenge against this crowd. Half of them were twice my size—which wasn't hard to accomplish at my measly five foot three. However, it had been the guides that had fascinated me. They were all bold and intimidating and each wore formal dress clothes of gray and black. Normally, I would have said the style was too dull, but I had a new appreciation for colors not found in the rainbow lately. The little flashes of color in the form of symbols and the awesome accessories made the simple styles more dramatic. Molly's symbol was red and shaped like an arrow with wings.

Devon explained that each contestant would be pledged as a Potential to one of the six Paldimori Houses. Each house was identified by a symbol and had a ruler—or Kyrion. The Kyrion operated by three rules: 1) all contestants were under the Kyrion's protection; 2) they couldn't help a contestant once the competitions started unless there was a unanimous vote; 3) no fornicating with contestants.

The guides were there to train the contestants and could not provide any assistance without permission from the Kyrion.

We were each given a torque necklace and told to wear it at all times. Then lined up and marched in a really dismal parade. I would have recommended balloon animals, but I didn't think this overly serious crowd would appreciate my trying to liven up their ceremony.

We were led to an awe-inspiring grand rotunda, and, as we crossed the floor to stop on our assigned symbols in front of a stage with six black thrones, the ballroom scene from

Beauty and the Beast played through my head and made me want to dance.

A huge black statue with white eyes stood in the middle of the platform. Smaller, less intimidating-looking statues of men and women stood behind each of the thrones, holding the House symbols.

Sitting on the thrones were figures draped in cloaks of different colors with their hoods pulled down low over their faces. Moonlight spilled from an opening in the ceiling far above, making creepy shadows shift around them. They were like a colorful council of grim reapers and I half-expected pipe music from *Phantom of the Opera* to start playing. I would have applauded them for dissing the black robes, but I was too busy trying not to scratch like I had a bad case of poison ivy.

A draft of cold air hit me, which then shifted to warm—back and forth making the hairs on my body dance. It was similar to the ripples that Lia sent out but cranked up to bone-jarring intensity. It was only my trust in Lia and my need to win the prize that Jaxon had dangled before me that kept me standing there.

Lia had promised that this wasn't a corporate retreat—which would've made me break out in hives from all the dull colors and politically correct conversations. But she hadn't warned me about the gamma radiation or whatever it was that was affecting me. She'd told me to stand there and pledge to do my best in the games and don't tell anyone anything about my time here. Yep, I could do that. Right now, would be good, before I stripped down and started trying to scratch at my itches like a flea-infested dog. I twisted my pink skirt nervously with clammy hands, wishing that Lia would have been allowed to be here with me.

Words were being exchanged around me, but I couldn't concentrate. I squirmed and scanned the room for an escape route. Then the throned figure in the white robe dropped her hood to reveal a black-haired beauty with the brightest blue eyes I'd ever seen, and I almost sighed in relief as the buzzing on my skin stopped. Suddenly, a jolt—like electricity—shot through the air and snapped my spine straight. Luckily, it wasn't as strong as what I had experienced earlier, and I was able to push it away with some deep-breathing yoga exercises.

My focus was drawn to the woman on the throne. She pushed her robe aside to show off an impressive set of breasts that were practically tumbling from her low-cut white dress. Her plump red lips curled into a seductive smile as she leaned toward Chris, his glasses askew and dirty-blonde hair a mess. I could practically hear his heavy gulp from across the room as more of those perfectly tanned breasts spilled forward.

"You can call me Nyx," she purred "and I will possibly answer." She sat back in her seat with a satisfied smirk.

Molly dropped to her knees in front of me facing the throne with the red cloak. "Ruler of the House of Arrows, I gift you a champion."

A rich velvet voice I knew all too well issued from beneath the hood. "What is your name, tiny peacock?"

The nickname irritated me, but a warm breeze was washing over my skin like a long-lost lover. Desire pooled in my belly quick and hot. My voice came out high and squeaky when I said, "Dia King."

That velvet voice purred mockingly, "I think you mean Potential Dia King. Is that not right?"

Something moved under the skin along my back. Before I could answer, cold enveloped me like I'd jumped into the

Arctic Ocean. Shivers wracked through me, but I tried to keep my focus. "R-Right."

"Do you think a pretty little girl like you could be a worthy champion for my House, Dia?"

"I'm w-worthy," I bit out through gritted teeth, trying to keep them from chattering.

The cold settled deeper into my bones, and it felt like I was seconds from collapsing into hypothermia. Then the hood was gone, and I was staring up into Jaxon's too-beautiful face. Those dark blue eyes locked with mine and that warm breeze from earlier swept back in to thaw me out. It wrapped around me, then sank into my core, where it felt as though the door to a hidden room had edged open. Jaxon's grin slipped for a moment. He pushed halfway up from his chair, then seemed to catch himself and settled back in a sprawl.

Then that smirk was back. Great Mother, it was irritating and sexy at the same time. The debonair lawyer had been replaced by an unrepentant sex god whose grin invited me to indulge in every fantasy I'd ever had. His eyes told me he could make every one of them come true. He ran his tongue over his bottom lip, and immediately my gaze followed that shiny path. Lust filled me with images of that sexy mouth on my body. Of my legs wrapped around that lean waist as we both cried out in ecstasy. My lips were suddenly parched, and I knew without a doubt he was the only one that could quench my thirst.

Danger! Danger! Flirt-mode engaged. Evasive maneuvers. I cocked my head to the side and gave him a puzzled 'does-that-usually-work?' look. His smile faded into confusion. *Guess what? I'm still not falling for your charm.* This girl isn't a disposable bed warmer.

He was like a great white and I was a guppy. If I let him

get too close, he would swallow me whole. I didn't know how to play his games, and I didn't want to know. He was the Male Model of the Year and a hotshot lawyer. I was an ex-teacher who talked to her cat more than people and loved to decorate my clothes in interesting ways. Still, I found myself fascinated by this disparity. I would never admit it, but I had spent way too many hours online researching him. The internet had been filled with mouth-watering photos of his modeling career and pictures of him with dozens of women. The one thing I couldn't find was anything about his career as a lawyer.

"You are right, tiny peacock. You will serve me—"

A throat cleared somewhere to the left, and Jaxon grinned.

"You will serve *my* House well. I will personally see to it. I accept what fate intends, Potential King of the House of Arrows. You may call me Eros—or, my god—and I will answer."

Our eyes locked. His gleamed with an unholy promise.

I'm in so much trouble.

9

A boy of five or six was seated on a giant black throne with his feet dangling over the edge. A black crown topped a riot of messy black curls. One small hand rested on the head of a red-and-black dragon the size of a little horse. It leaned over the boy, its wings draped around the throne as if it would wrap him up in its scaly embrace and protect him from the world. The boy's sapphire eyes stared vacantly out over the large group of people who knelt before him. He looked so alone, even in their midst, sitting there completely silent and still like a statue.

Three more thrones lay to his left and two to his right. The beauty of the men and women upon those seats threatened to overwhelm my senses. The pearlescent glow of the women's skin contrasted with the various tanned shades of the men. Their eyes gleamed in the dim light of the cave, like gems ranging from the most vivid emerald to a smoke-gray jade. They wore simple clothing—all in black like the rest of the crowd—and yet they somehow outshone everything around them. Only the nearly imperceptible slump to their shoulders hinted at a weariness that added vulnerability to these otherwise intimidating people.

It was the colors surrounding them that fascinated me the

most. *Every person there was ringed in color like an aura, but the people on the thrones had that ripple effect—like Lia. My heartbeat seemed to follow the ebb and flow of those ripples, gaining in speed. When it felt like they would pound right through my rib cage, a static charge shot through me causing every hair on my body to rise.*

My eyes were drawn to the little boy. He was surrounded by a swirling wall of colors that spread several feet around him. There was something else moving in that wall of colors, but as hard as I squinted, I couldn't get a good view. Without even realizing what I was doing, I reached out as if to touch him and my back arched in a silent scream. There was a churning river of emotions pouring into me. Anger. Weariness. Regret. Fear. Pain. Pain. PAIN!

I was caught in an undertow of emotions. I kicked and fought, but it kept dragging me under. Then a thunderous voice echoed through the roughly hewn cave, and I was yanked free.

"The winter solstice is once more upon us. We have sailed the Earth and finally found our sanctuary just as Titan bid us. Our bodies are travel-weary and our hearts heavy with loss. Yet, we have much work to do. The world we knew is gone. We will build a stronger world. A world where our children will be safe."

I wanted to wake up, but I felt frozen in place. My arms were covered in goose bumps from the cold. My bare feet shuffled on the hard rock trying to find warmth, grains of dirt chaffing at my soles. Who were these people? What were they doing here? What had just happened to me?

The boy's swirling eyes collided with mine and that thunderous voice issued from his open mouth. "The dawn of a new era is upon us. Today we build anew. From this day forward, we will be known as the Paldimori."

I bolted upright in bed. Clouds of steam hung suspended in the air with each rapid breath. I was so cold that my skin felt tight, as if it might shatter if I moved too quickly. Slowly I scooted to the edge of the large round bed. Stinging prickles covered my whole body—like when your arm goes to sleep. Slowly, I made my way to the bathroom and stepped into the shower, not even bothering to remove my sleep shirt. I gasped as the lukewarm water rained down on me like needles piercing into my skin.

I slumped forward and rested my forehead against the wall. "Even my dreams have turned dark and gloomy."

It was a long while before I finally got warm enough. I dragged myself from the shower and pulled off the soaked shirt. Then dressed in my favorite yoga outfit—a neon-pink halter top and psychedelic capris. It was too early for someone who didn't like mornings, but I was wired after that strange dream. I raided the fridge for some yogurt and added in a handful of Skittles. Bless whoever had stocked a whole drawer of them!

I walked to the wall of windows that formed the backdrop to the sunken living room. The shadowed valley far below was slowly revealed in orange and rose tones as the sun peeked over the horizon. If only I had my paints to capture the magic of this place. Everywhere I looked there was a feast for my artistic senses. From the mesmerizing beauty of the landscape to the fascinating diversity of people. To the neo-classical paintings of battle scenes and naked women that decorated the walls of my floor here in Titan Tower. The paintings weren't really my style, but the skill of the artist was incomparable. Maybe I would brave Molly's wrath and ask for paint supplies.

As the sun climbed higher over the horizon, I started my routine. I had discovered my love of yoga during college. It had helped me to deal with my aversion to mornings and to find my focus when my brain didn't want to shut down.

Most people thought I was a ditz with too much air in my head and not enough brain cells. The truth was that my mind never stopped. It was like having the city that never sleeps inside your head. The only way I could deal with the constant noise and bustle was through yoga.

I breathed deeply and exhaled all of the tension. My focus shifted to the tightening of every muscle as I worked through the positions. My mind was clear and my soul at ease for the first time in a while as I hung in a wide-legged forward bend. A choked cough cut through my concentration and I opened my eyes to find "Eros" standing a few feet behind me. His gaze locked with my upside-down one as a blinding smile spread across his face.

"Now you're only teasing me. I hate to inform Lia, but she's just lost her crown. You in this position is now my new favorite way to be greeted. I can't believe you've been hiding *that* under those bulky skirts." He grumbled as if his powers of seeking out prime female body parts had failed him. "But my hands are always available if you would like a partner to help *support* you."

The heavy weight of his gaze penetrated my calm making me rush through the last couple of positions. I ignored him as I wiped the sweat from my face and arms with a small towel. Then gulped down a bottle of water. I had hoped that he would take the hint that I wanted to be alone, but when I turned he was laying on the couch built into the step-down of the living room. His head propped on his hand as he watched me. His feet were bare. His red T-shirt and worn jeans hugged his lean swimmer's body. There was something in his expression—like he had a secret that was bursting to be shared—but he didn't say anything.

"Didn't the rules say something about you not being allowed in my rooms?" I asked.

"I'm not allowed to be in your bedroom. Unless you invite me, of course." That sexy grin captured my attention. Those full lips pulled down into a cute little pout. "Invite me to your bedroom, Dia. Pretty please. I promise you that every inch of your body will thank me."

"Do women fall for this?" My hands trembled as I pulled the scrunchie from my hair and combed my fingers through it to distract myself from the lust pouring through me.

"I don't have to try this hard with most women," he stated as he gracefully got to his feet and walked toward me. His eyes tracked my hands as I continued to finger-comb the mess I had created by putting my hair up wet. "I can't remember the last time I pursued a woman. Maybe Becky Sims in fifth grade. She had the best snacks. It took the whole lunch break to convinced her we were dating and, as a good girlfriend, she should share her snacks."

"You bribed a girl out of her lunch by promising her dates?"

"She had Little Debbie snacks," he said as if that justified everything.

"What kind?"

Jaxon stepped in front of me then leaned in to whisper slowly, "Strawberry Shortcake Rolls."

My mouth watered, and I groaned. "How dare she bring that yummy goodness to school and not share!"

"Exactly. She was torturing me." His fingers traced my cheek. "That spongy cake layer ..." Then trailed down to brush my lips. "... the rich creme that melts on your tongue." My tongue darted out before I knew what was happening and his rich taste hit me. "... the sweet–tart layer of strawberry." His finger dipped into my mouth to follow my tongue.

"Delicious," he breathed as his lips glided lightly against mine. My breath caught. My eyes fluttered closed as he hovered there drawing out the moment until all I wanted to do was grab him and pull his lips to mine.

Then he was across the room and walking to the elevator door. How did he get over there so quickly?

"It's time to start training." The gruffness of his voice was the only indication he had been as affected by that almost-kiss as I was.

10

Jaxon had acted like he was afraid to get near me on the ride down to the training floor. He had left me at the elevator doors saying he had something to look into. The only people I saw were Devon and Maya who looked to be having a battle of wills as they glared at each other. Instead of going in the direction Jaxon had pointed out to get to the gym, I went the opposite way, deciding I had time to explore.

The training floor was a massive cave that looked like an insane interior decorator had pieced together stage settings for all four of the elements. There was a forest area for earth. A large lagoon area for water. A scary-looking section of rock pillars that glowed an angry red was fire. And two slender towers surrounded by rushing wind. There were other areas too, but I didn't stop to check them out.

When I arrived at the gym area, Molly was already there looking angry and ready to rip into me. Then I noticed her eyes dart over to the man and woman sparring on the mats. Lia was here! I rushed over happy to see her, but before I could reach her Bennett took advantage of her distraction to tag her. She said something, and he scooped her up. She shouted to me that she would see me at dinner as he carried her toward the elevator. The excitement I had felt at finally getting to spend some time with her died. She had promised she would be here with me through this. It looked like I was on my own.

I turned to Molly, surprised to see a look of pain on her face as she watched Lia leave as well. *What had happened between those two?* Before I could ask, Molly started snapping out instructions. She pushed my limits, but I took up the challenge and made it my own. If Molly declared we were doing burpees, I added a Malasana pose—or yoga squat. It wasn't about trying to crack that tough shell of hers —I considered the fact that Molly had yelled at me for a solid five minutes as progress—but I needed to win this. My whole life was hanging in the balance.

By the time I took second place in the three-mile foot race, I was exhausted, but feeling a little lighter. Slowly the edges of the crater that losing Dan and my job had left in my life were being filled with new purpose. I could do this.

I went up to my room and was surprised to find Lia there waiting for me. For the first time since we had literally run into each other in college, I didn't know how to act around her. Lia had been the only other constant in my life besides Dan. She had been through a lot, and I had allowed her to be the one to determine how much she was willing to share of what had happened to her. She had finally told me about the boating accident with her parents a couple of months ago. She'd also promised that she was going to try harder to open up to me, but she was rarely around anymore. When she was, she seemed more and more different.

She hugged me and apologized for not being able to be with me until now. I shrugged it off like it was no big deal, but that wasn't the way it felt. Lia followed me to the bathroom talking about how great I was doing. She was still talking when I hopped in the shower. It was funny how our roles seemed reversed right now. She was the one talking non-stop and all in love. I was the one holding back and having no luck in love.

"Damn, Dia, you almost beat that asshole Mikhail in the race today," Lia shouted to be heard over the shower. "How come I've never seen you run like that?"

"Probably because you're allergic to exercise," I shouted back while trying to keep shampoo suds out of my mouth.

"Hey, I can't help it if I have an allergy," she exclaimed in defense. "People should thank me for not putting them in harm's way."

"You *are* more accident prone than Wile E. Coyote in a gym." I finished rinsing and turned off the shower. "What do you think would have happened if the Road Runner had been a girl? She probably would have brought in a bear. And been all like 'come get some grub.' Nom nom. The end."

"Don't hate on the coyote. Watching him get blown up by his own traps was the only thing that kept me sane that summer I was bedridden."

"That must be where your love of action movies came from."

"What can I say? Chaos and mayhem are kinda my things. You could even say Chaos is my superpower," Lia said with a chuckle. "I've given up on the cape, though. My time as Dominatrix Girl in the first competition ruined my interest in costumes."

I dried off and slipped into a peasant shirt and harem pants. Then walked to the sink where Lia sat on the counter swinging her legs. Her long mahogany hair was pulled up in a high ponytail. Her red V-neck *Star Wars* T-shirt had a picture of Princess Leia on it and said: *Don't Mess with a Princess*. The shirt was more form-fitting than usual, as were her jeans. They both showed off a well-endowed Romanesque body that left men panting, unlike my own nonexistent curves.

She was humming—something I hadn't heard her do in a long time. I had been forced into enough movie marathons with her to recognize the *Star Wars* theme song. For some strange reason, she was obsessed with those movies. I had never been a fan. Give me cartoons or romance. Happy endings were my soul food.

I dug into my messenger bag and pulled out my brush, prepared to tackle my Rapunzel-like hair.

"Here, let me." Lia jumped off the counter and took my brush. She sectioned the damp tresses that skimmed my thighs and started working through the tangles. Our reflections were a sharp contrast in the mirror. She was the tall all-American beauty with porcelain skin that I had longed for as a child. I looked like an exotic waif with my olive-toned skin and large azure-blue eyes. She was my opposite in every way, but there was no one else in the world I had ever felt closer to.

Or I had at one time.

"Thanks," I said around the lump in my throat.

"I haven't done this since we were in college." Lia's eyes met my teary gaze in the mirror. "I meant what I said about being a better friend, Dia."

There were things I wanted to say, but my throat closed up on me.

She swallowed thickly, her own eyes teary but didn't say anything more. I watched silently as she worked over my hair. I had held on tight to the image of the girl I knew from college. I'd safely preserved that memory of who she had been as if she would one day pick it back up like a favorite shirt. But seeing her now, I knew that Lia was long gone.

Pain bit into my chest—the feeling I was losing her all over again.

She was creating a new life for herself, one with Bennett. One without me. I needed to let the image of who I wanted her to be go. I pictured that bright-eyed girl who knew she could take on the world and win. I mentally wrapped her up in a giant hug and whispered, "*Goodbye, College Lia, I'm going to miss you.*"

Her image faded away.

But even if we were different people now, I had to believe our friendship would last. She was the sister of my heart. Losing Lia completely would be the last blow to crumble my battered heart. Determination filled me.

Hello, New Lia, it's nice to meet you.

She bumped my hip, pulling me from my thoughts, "Are you ok?

"Yeah, I think I will be."

"I'm here if you want to talk," Lia said cautiously, "We could have a sleepover like we used to?"

"I think I'd like that."

"Great." The excited smile she gave me brought a little bit of color back to my world.

11

The same black-haired boy from my dream last night sat atop the black-and-red dragon. His eyes swirled with colors, but there was no mistaking the pain in their depths. He held out his hand toward me. On his palm was a large emerald that glowed, lighting up his haggard face.

The emerald called to me like a siren song. It whispered to me that it belonged with me. That I was its true owner. That we needed each other. I craved it and tears slipped down my cheeks as I struggle to be reunited with the stone. But no matter how hard I tried, I couldn't move.

Cold crept up around my bare ankles and up my calves. When I looked down I saw frost climbing up my legs. I shivered in my sleep shirt. The sound of millions of cries pushed against me. I covered my ears, but it couldn't block out the sound. I searched for the boy, wanting him to make it stop. His eyes settled into a startling sapphire-blue color and, for a moment, his face morphed from that of a young boy to a man's. Then darkness began to swirl around him and the swirling colors slowly bled back into his eyes to take over the blue. His face contorted in agony and the boy was back.

A single bright blue tear slid down his cheek before the darkness swallowed him.

My eyes opened to darkness with a shout on the tip of my tongue. For a moment, I thought I was stuck in the dark with the boy, but then I saw moonlight coming from the bedroom window. Slowly, I sat up on the side of the bed and put my head in my hands. It wasn't unusual for my dreams to be filled with people and places I'd never seen before. But this felt different. I didn't know why but this dream had felt like a possibility. Like a premonition of something that could happen. My stomach clenched thinking of that darkness.

I walked over to the windows. The moon was nearly full and hung high over the valley below. A glimmer of light on a ridge top in the distance caught my attention. What was that? Movement at the base of my spine had me spinning around, but the room was empty. That dream must have affected me more than I realized. Then I felt it again and, with it, came a tugging sensation. Almost, like what I had felt for the emerald in my dream, but not as intense.

I rubbed the base of my spine and closed my eyes trying to figure out where the tugging was coming from. Moments later, I heard the chime of the elevator.

Great Mother Earth, how had I gotten here?

I was standing right outside the elevator—in a jungle. At least, that was my guess, since I was surrounded by the heavy weight of humid air and the damp scent of earth. Not to mention the towering trees and riot of animal sounds. Sweat beaded my skin already. The sun was bright in the projected sky. The transition from night that I had seen outside my window to this artificial day was jarring. That tugging sensation flared up again. I was an adventurer, it was in my DNA, but even I knew it would be a bad idea to go into the jungle by myself.

I turned to get back on the elevator and shrieked. I scrambled backwards and fell onto my butt. Grass tickled the backs of my thighs as my sleep shirt bunched up around my waist. My messenger bag tangled around me, I hadn't even known I was carrying it. A giant crab stood in front of the elevator. It was easily three feet tall with pincers as big as dinner plates. Its plated body was splashed with blues and purples, and reddish-brown patches down its six segmented legs. Its antennae waved in the air as its dark red eyes watched me from the end of their stalks.

It was kinda ugly-cute. The colors were pretty, but weren't bright colors a sign that something was poisonous? I slowly untangled myself from my bag and started to stand. The crab took a step closer. I stopped moving and it did too. I tried again with the same results. Ok, we were at a *shell*mate.

"Uh, hey, I didn't mean to invade your space," I said to the giant crab. "Yeah, so, if you want to just move a little to the side, I can leave."

The crab's claws made clacking sounds as they opened and closed rapidly. I gulped and braced myself for an attack. It scuttled forward, and I jumped to my feet. I got into a self-defense stance and waited. One big claw reached out and bumped my bag. The it did it again. "You want my bag?"

The claw eased forward, and the strap of my bag was between those claws. "Hey, you don't have to break it." My hand contacted the edge of the claw and impressions came to me in the same way as with Mr. Skittles.

Color. Shine. Mine. Color. Shine. Mine. Goddess.

A smile stretched across my lips and I laughed. I was Dr.

Doolittle. "You can have the bag. But you have to promise to let me leave after I give it to you. Ok?"

Stay. Belong. Show. Goddess.

What did that mean? A rustling sound came from the woods behind me. Then the chittering of monkeys. I loved animals, but this was looking more like a *When Animals Attack!* episode. I slipped the bag over my head and dropped it in front of the crab. "It's all yours. Remember our deal?"

Instead of taking the bag, it nudged me with the back side of its claw. I stumbled back a step. A glance over my shoulder showed monkeys peering at me from the tree line. This was an alternate universe where the animals herded the human. I put my hand back on the crab-thing to communicate, but I was suddenly knocked off my feet. A solid weight pushed me into the ground. Heavy breathing brushed my ear and my training kicked in.

I reached both hands behind my head as I pulled my knees up and used my hips as leverage to flip the person off me. I quickly rolled in the opposite direction and got to my feet. The forest was unnaturally silent.

"I stand—or I guess 'lie' would be the proper word at the moment—corrected," Jaxon said, his voice full of amusement. "You aren't a peacock, you're a tiger in disguise. Mind giving me a hand up, Tigerlily?"

"I have a name," I grumbled as I offered him a hand. "You probably flirt with so many women you don't remember it."

"I remember everything about you, Tigerlily," he grinned. "Some parts more fondly than others."

He flashed me a teasing smile as he took my hand and tugged. I landed on top of him with a grunt.

"What're you doing?" I struggled in his hold and managed to get into a sitting position.

"Talking," he said as his large hands gripped my thighs.

Oh, this was bad. I straddled his hips. The hardness beneath me wasn't all muscle. Heat crept across my chest and Jaxon laughed at my reaction. My traitorous body urged me to take advantage of our positions, and I had to think of yoga to keep my hips from moving.

"W-We can talk just fine standing," I gulped. "Uh, like on opposite sides of the jungle."

"This is the Emerald Rain Forest." He watched me patiently as if waiting for something and he had all the time in the world. "I'm not sure how you even found this floor, but you are always full of surprises." I tried to move off him, but he gripped me tighter. "What's your hurry? I find this a very comfortable position to talk in."

"I don't think so." I struggled again, but that only seemed to make things worse. The hardness underneath the fly of his jeans grew bigger. His grip on my hips tightened, pulling me more firmly against that ridge. My breath trembled out of me as he rubbed against me through the thin layer of my panties.

"So, uh, do you think if a tree falls in the woods it still makes a noise?" I squeaked out, trying to distract us both. "I bet yes. Animals would hear it. Owls have excellent hearing, you know. So do cats. Mr. Skittles one day heard me open a pack of Skittles all the way downstairs, and I was really quiet."

Jaxon was laughing, but a deeper laugh joined in from behind me. I glanced over my shoulder to find a smiling Bennett and a very angry-looking Lia.

"I think your friend is fine," Bennett said.

Lia stomped over to us. "Having fun, Jaxon?"

"Yes," he smirked, "could you maybe not ruin the moment? You tend to be a bad influence."

"No way, that's my best friend you're trying to sex-up." Lia grabbed my hand and pulled me off him. "She's way too innocent to be left alone with you."

Heat crept over my chest. "Geez, I'm not a kid. We were just ... talking."

"Exactly." Lia said, then gave Jaxon the "I'm-watching-you" gesture. She turned to me. "Why are you here?"

"Whoa, what's going on?" I asked. Instead of answering me, she glanced around the area. I had a feeling that my bestie wasn't telling me something. Again. My heart ached, but I told myself to give it time. "Hey, did you see where that crab went to?"

"Do you mean Phil?" Bennett asked as he wrapped his arm around Lia.

"Uh, maybe? There was this giant crab with pretty purple and blue colors." I looked around again, but there was nothing except us. "He was blocking the elevator."

Jaxon stepped closer. "He's a coconut crab. A *huge* coconut crab thanks to Molly feeding him all the time. He's harmless."

Lia elbowed Bennett in the stomach. Then snuggled into his arms. "You named a giant crab Phil?"

"It is a fitting name." Bennett pulled Lia tight against him. "He often comes to the elevator doors when anyone visits. Phil is an excellent doorman."

"Only you would have a giant crab as a door greeter, wacky wizard." Lia pushed out of Bennett's arms and walked toward the elevator. Bennett narrowed his eyes and, a second later, she yelped, rubbing her butt. She glared at him over her shoulder. "Not nice."

Bennett stalked after her and I looked away. Jealousy was an ugly emotion that I wasn't used to feeling.

I looked around the area once more. "I think Phil took my bag."

Jaxon helped me search, but we didn't find any sign of it. "They're called 'robber crabs' for a reason. He lives over there in the roots of that group of trees." Jaxon pointed to a dense group of massive trees in the distance. "We can go search and give those two some privacy."

Bennett's deep voice cut in. "A servant can be sent later. Dinner will be served soon, and the Kyrion are hosting tonight."

Lia cleared her throat. "Yeah, that means they're going to invite the peasants up to the Kyrion floors to wow them with their fancy digs. Then bore us to tears with another ceremony. Run while you can, Dia."

"I would, but a klepto crab is probably doing drag with the only bra I brought with me," I sighed. "How formal is this dinner?"

12

Candlelight danced on the river-rock walls of the dining room. Huge candle chandeliers hung from the arched ceiling above. Large paintings of the same men and women portrayed in the smaller statues in the throne room lined the walls. Beyond the three open arches at the end of the room, people stood at long tables intently focused on preparing numerous dishes for the meal. A fire roared in a large fireplace at the center of the back wall where meats cooked on spits. Women in black jumpsuits climbed tall ladders to pluck herbs from pots that covered the rest of the wall from floor to ceiling.

Two long tables lined opposite sides of the huge dining room. The guides and Kyrion sat at one table. The contestants sat at the other with their groups of four servants, all in black, standing behind their chairs. Molly had explained that these were volunteers who had won their assignment through some rite of passage. They were the personal servants for their Potentials during the Games. With their consent, they could also be one of the prizes that a contestant could choose after winning a training session. I'd avoided the four men standing behind me like the plague since learning that.

Nikki didn't seem to have the same problem. She giggled from her spot a couple of seats down from me as one of her servants pressed an apricot to her mouth. One fanned her with a large palm frond. The other two massaged her hands. Our seats were spaced widely apart, but I still heard the snort from beside me. Kade seemed to be one of the few men immune to her.

A gray-haired man in all black stepped through the middle archway with an honest-to-goodness set of wooden panpipes pressed to his lips. A high note trilled through the room quieting the conversations.

Bennett stood from his seat. His black suit did nothing to hide the hard muscles underneath, and I hid my smile as Lia surreptitiously eyed his butt. "We have known tragedy and our hearts still ache with the loss of one of our own. But the Games must go on. The Gods have blessed us with Potentials to fulfill our sworn duty. Erebus will lead us in this next competition. I ask you all to remain vigilant and report any suspicious behavior to your Kyrion immediately. May the Gods guide and protect us all."

Glasses were raised in toast, but I was distracted. What had he meant by all of that? Who had died?

The panpipes sounded again, interrupting my thoughts, and a procession of people filed through the archways loaded down with food. My mouth watered as a plate filled with a five-star-looking meal was set in front of me. I cut into the steak and groaned at the taste that burst across my tongue. A familiar warm breeze caressed my bare shoulders, and I knew he was watching me. I sipped my water trying to quench my suddenly parched throat. Over the rim of my glass, my eyes locked with a pair of midnight-blue ones.

Jaxon sprawled in his chair looking every bit the sex symbol he was. A wicked smile spread across those sinful lips that could tempt a saint. The flickering light from the candelabras on the table played along the planes of his high cheekbones and stubbled jaw. Several buttons were open on his red shirt showing off smooth muscles that rippled as his eyes dipped to where I was tugging again at the neckline of my borrowed dress.

I shifted in the plush black chair as lust bloomed in my core. My bag had been found and returned to me earlier. But my bra had been missing. That might not have been such a problem if I'd been able to wear my own clothes, but Molly had declared my wardrobe unfit for anything except a hippie convention. Then called in her cousin who loaned me this dress. The square neckline of the red slip dress kept sliding down threatening to flash what little goods I had at everyone. That wasn't the kind of dinner show anyone wanted to see.

Well, not most people anyway. For a moment, the wind played tug-of-war with my dress, and I could almost hear Jaxon encouraging me to let it slip.

Dinner went by slowly, feeling like torture as I felt Jaxon's gaze on me several times. Then the dishes were cleared away and there was dancing. Somehow Bennett got Lia to dance and didn't lose a limb in the process. I watched them twirl around the room, lost in each other. They were beautiful together and so much in love. My heart ached with longing to find the love and family I'd always wanted.

My mother was all the family I'd ever known until Lia. I'd spent many hours of my childhood on the rooftop of our apartment building dreaming out loud to the flowers. Sometimes I dreamed that mom and I were reunited with her tribe who had been searching for us since she left. Other times I dreamed that Prince Charming came to take me away on his white horse, and we lived happily ever after surrounded by a dozen kids. But those were just fantasies. Real life was like the tide: slowly pulling the sand from beneath your feet.

I exhaled shakily when I realized what I'd been thinking. My mother had struggled to find her feet after my father left us, and I'd watched as she sank deeper into a dark place I couldn't understand. I was stronger than that.

You can get other jobs. You can fall in love again. Nothing is impossible when you have hope.

"Ma'am, are you ok?" Kade asked.

"Oh, yeah, fine." I relaxed my fisted hands and forced a yawn. "Long day."

Kade searched my face, his baby blue eyes filled with a kindness that said he saw through my lie. "I'm an ok listener. At least, that's what my sister says."

Maya, on my other side, huffed. "As I expected. You are weak." I turned to her, my mouth hanging open in shock as she continued on matter-of-factly. "I calculated your chances of winning the Games at 3.4627%."

"Uh ..." Was she a robot disguised as an Asian accountant? That boring pantsuit looked creased sharp enough to cut someone. "That's not too bad, right? I have better odds than whoever's at zero."

"You *were* at zero." Her black eyes raked over me clinically. "I gave you back points for being best friends with Chaos's girlfriend. That gives you a slight advantage."

"Don't listen to her, ma'am," Kade cut in. "Her heart's a calculator. People can't be figured out with an equation. You'll do just fine."

"Thanks." I gave him a quick smile. Right now, I would

love to be curled up on my couch with Mr. Skittles, watching a favorite movie.

I started to excuse myself when a flash of red caught my eye. Jaxon walked toward me, determination in every stride. His eyes locked on me like a target and, for the first time, I didn't see a shred of the playboy in his expression. I gulped, curious and scared at the same time about what would happen when he reached me. Suddenly, Nikki sprang up out of nowhere and gripped his arm before he could get too far. Her painted-on floral sundress hugged every curve as she leaned into him. Her fingers trailed down his chest as she stood on tiptoe to whisper in his ear. Jaxon's eyes never left mine as he responded to her. When she traced a finger along his jaw, his eyes narrowed, and he leaned down to whisper to her.

An icy cold tingle started at the base of my spine and spread across my back. Goose bumps pebbled my skin, and my breath steamed the air. Several people around me rubbed their arms and moved away uneasily. I gripped the table edge as something seemed to grow deep inside me. I trembled in horror as my fingers started to sink down into the wood. The table groaned and began to shake.

I quickly pushed out of my chair and ran to the elevator. I made it to my floor and ran to the wall of windows. A full moon hung in the sky, its light barely penetrating the dense valley below. What was happening to me? Ever since I had come to this island, I had felt uncomfortable in my own skin. Not that I had ever truly felt comfortable. There was something broken in me. I'd learned long ago to be ok with my flaws. Some days were harder than others. But I didn't want to become like my mother.

I shivered again. These cold spells were getting worse. Not only that, but there was an incessant tugging sensation urging me beyond these walls. My eyes landed on a ridge in the distance. I needed to be there. *Now*.

Everything went sort of hazy and, the next thing I knew, I was standing barefoot in the middle of the Emerald Rain Forest. I gasped, shivering as the cold slowly seeped away.

"Go now."

"Who's there?" I twisted around looking for the owner of that whispered demand.

"Save them."

"Save who? Who are you?"

Mist swirled up from the forest floor at the base of a tree with massive roots that weaved across the ground like ribbons in all directions. The mist grew more substantial and took on the shape of a young girl. Pigtail braids hung down her chest from under a scarf. Her dress looked like a patchwork quilt that hung on her thin frame revealing knobby knees. She held out her hand, her large dark eyes begging me to take it. Just as my fingertips brushed the cold of hers, lightning struck her. An eerie howl of pain and frustration filled the air.

I stumbled backward shielding my eyes at the intense light before it faded away. The smell of ozone and burning leaves assaulted my nose. Tentatively, I approached the tree, stepping over the lines of bare dirt that snaked across the ground where the lightning had burned away the grass. A metal symbol of a lotus flower was embedded in the tree about waist-high at the juncture of the roots. It gave off a faint glow that seemed to get brighter as I brought my hand up next to it. In the dim light of the moon, projected on the ceiling above, I could see the matching symbol on my palm. My fingers traced the warm metal of the symbol on the tree, and a breeze blew back my hair. I shielded my eyes as the symbol grew brighter and brighter.

The crack of thunder sounded overhead. I looked up as lightning arced across the sky before shooting straight toward me. A scream ripped from my throat and my heart beat erratically as the electric current reached for me. Suddenly, I was pushed from behind.

I screamed again as my head made contact with the tree. But, instead of hitting rough bark, I hit air and went falling into darkness.

13

I fell for what seemed like hours before crashing into something hard. I bounced off, stumbling before my shaky legs gave out and collapsed to the ground. This was definitely not Sotiria. Somehow, I'd fallen down the rabbit hole and into the middle of a war.

A few dozen ramshackle huts sat in a clearing surrounded by thick woods. The humid air made each panted breath a struggle. The gray-blue of the evening sky was marred by plumes of smoke. Screams and shouts echoed through the clearing. Fires engulfed several of the huts. The earth trembled. Tree limbs danced a choreographed ballet above a tangle of people locked in battle, swooping in to land a blow here and there. Balls of fire sailed through the air igniting tree limbs and people alike. Water rushed across the ground from out of nowhere, drenching me.

Six and a half feet of solid muscle loomed over me. I'd run headlong into trouble, and he looked really angry. His olive T-shirt strained over bulging muscles. His black fatigue pants sported an array of weapons. Fire raged in his eyes. No, seriously—his irises danced with flames.

He took a step toward me, a ball of fire flared in his beefy palm. He drew back his hand, and I scrambled backward. A wagon wheel flew through the air like a frisbee and plowed into his gut. He grunted but kept stalking toward me. The wheel looped back around like a boomerang to hit him in the back. This time he stumbled, but it only made him angrier. The fire in his eyes leaped up to lick at his close-cropped hair. The wheel came back around, but he dropped to the ground, and it flew over his head to smash into a group of similarly dressed men.

The GI Joe-wannabe flipped back onto his feet and came at me again. A burst of wind swept past me and sent him smashing through the wall of a hut.

A hand wrapped around my mouth, muffling my scream. "It's me," Jaxon said. "We have to move."

We ducked and weaved through the battle zone as the bronze-skinned villagers in their raggedy clothes faced off against the military-like forces. I tripped over the scorched body of a woman, and strong hands roughly pulled me upright before I fell on top of her. Those sightless wide eyes and the smell of her charred flesh hit me like a punch. I turned away and doubled over gagging.

Tears streamed down my cheeks. What in the name of the Great Mother is going on? Who are these people?

Strong arms wrapped around me and Jaxon lifted me off my feet. The wind whistled by as we moved so fast my head spun. We entered one of the thatched huts. Moonlight seeped through a hole in the roof revealing a single room with a pallet bed and a few scattered pots. I was glad for the reprieve from the bloodbath outside. My heart was pounding madly, and I was ready to pee my pants in terror.

"Are you ok?"

"I'm—" I swallowed thickly. My head was shaking and then nodding. Ok wasn't even registering at the moment. "How did we get here? What's happening? Jaxon people are *dying*! The rain forest ... there was a g-ghost ... the tree ... fire eyes ..."

"Shhh. Shhh. I've got you. Deep breaths. In and out." Jaxon's arms tightened around me and, for a moment, we focused on breathing. I shivered in my wet dress, and he pulled me even closer. "That's it. Good girl. You're safe, Dia. I won't let anything happen to you."

He set me on my feet, still keeping me in the circle of his arms. His hands cupped my cheeks, his eyes peering into mine like he could see inside me. There was a strange blue outline to his eyes that seemed to be glowing and growing bigger. His throat worked for a moment as his thumbs smoothed over my cheeks. There was something like awe, tinged with nervousness, in his expression. "I need you to stay calm for me. Can you do that?"

I nodded.

"Good. That's good, sweetheart," he said almost absently.

I trembled against him as multiple explosions rocked the hut.

"I lost sight of you for a moment. I thought you were dead." His voice rasped with emotion as his hands tightened on my cheeks. Fierce determination hardened his features. "We will definitely be talking later. But I've got to get you out of here now. You should never have had to see this."

He bit out words in a lilting language, then said more to himself, "How the hell did you find a portal? I thought they were all destroyed. Well, except for the one in— Never-mind."

"Those people"—my voice shook, and I swallowed down the panic—"we've got to help them."

Jaxon tilted his head like he was listening to something. "The cavalry has arrived. They'll help the villagers. Right now, we're sitting in the middle of the war zone. We could be taken out by either side by accident if we don't get out of here."

"Why are those people attacking the village?"

Bitterness seeped from Jaxon's voice. "For power. Because they want to rule. Because they're bigots who hate my people for being who we are. Take your pick."

"Your *people*?"

"Paldimori isn't a corporation. It's the name of my people —our people. I can't—" Jaxon pulled me against him and crashed his mouth down on mine.

The GI Joe man from earlier kicked in the door to the hut. I cried out against Jaxon's lips and tried to pull away. We had to run! Instead of letting me go, Jaxon wrapped me tighter and kissed me deeper. His lips bruised mine as the man entered the hut. Blood dripped from his machete as his cold gaze swept the room. He swung the blade violently, cutting deep into the wood of the wall as he let out a growl of frustration. The he was gone.

Jaxon's lips gentled, and he slowly pulled away. The blue ring around his eyes pulsed in time with his heart thudding against my hand. "I can't mask us for much longer," he said gruffly. "I need to be fully charged in case we have to fight our way out. Do you remember the tree we came out of?"

"Huh?" I was still dazed from that kiss and having GI Joe walk right past us. "What just happened?"

"I don't have to time explain. Add it to the list of things we need to talk about."

"I can tell that list is going to get really long." I hadn't been keeping tally, but I was now. "You wanted to know about the tree, right? I was a bit busy trying not to break my head on GI Joe's keg to remember one tree when we're surrounded by a forest."

He was silent for a moment. "Keg?"

"You know, way more than a six-pack. His muscles had muscles."

"Right." I could hear the grin in his voice. He released me and walked over to peek out the door. "Looks like GI Joe isn't the type to give up easily. I'll distract him while you try to find the tree. Can you do that?"

"Sure, find a special tree in the woods in the dark. No biggie." Sarcasm dripped from me. "Any suggestions?"

"Do what you did before." He grabbed my hand, pulling me to him again, and kissed me so deep my toes curled. "For luck."

"How'm I supposed to think straight when you do that?"

He laughed, then threw the door open and raced outside. Crazy. He was crazy.

I lowered my voice in a poor mockery of his, "'*Just do what you did before.*' Like I even know!"

Ok, I can do this. It shouldn't be too hard to fall into some trees.

I huffed out a breath, then peeked out the door. Most of the fighting seemed to have moved to the other end of the village. Now or never. I eased out of the door and along the outer wall of the hut. A gust of wind nearly knocked me off my feet. The hut at my back shook as something heavy smashed into it. The wind howled again making the house groan and pop.

I raced across the open ground and into the trees. Here the sound of battle was dampened, the sudden change making the dark forest even more creepy. I rested for a moment against a tall tree, trying to get my bearings.

Which way do I go?

The tree had to have been near the edge of the forest given the way we were spat out into the clearing. At least, I hoped so. Staying several feet inside the tree line, I worked my way along.

A twig snapped. Shadows shifted.

I crouched down to hide, but it was too late. A knife pressed against my throat. Rapid fire words were hissed at me in a language I didn't recognize. Rustling announced the arrival of more people. A rough hand grabbed my bicep, pulling me to my feet. I could barely make out the dark-skinned face of a man with a beard. He gestured at me, getting irritated when I didn't answer.

I tried to act friendly. "I don't know what you're saying, but I hope it's 'I come in peace.'"

He frowned, then switched to an accented English. "You American?"

"That obvious, huh? Who are you?"

He ignored my question to speak to someone off to the side. Then turned back to me. "What you do here?"

"Sightseeing."

A chuckle came from behind me, but the man was not amused. "How you come here?"

"It's a long story involving a ghost, lightning, and a tree. Sounds like a B movie, but it's true." The knife pressed into my side. "Right, the Cliffs Notes version. I fell into a tree. More like through the tree and down a hole. Or was it inside the tree hole? Maybe—"

"Enough." He gripped my shoulders. "Where is tree?"

"Wish I knew. I can't say the tour had been that great.

Too much action and adventure. I'm more of a shopping and art museum kinda girl."

"I'll keep that in mind for our first date." Jaxon was suddenly beside us, flipping the knife end over end in one hand. A ball of light glowed from his left hand lighting up the scene around us. A small group of women and children huddled together a few feet away. Their fear was almost tangible. A teenage boy picked himself up off the ground and scowled at Jaxon.

"There won't be any first dates," I grumbled.

Jaxson smirked at me, then turned to the boy. "Lesson one, kid, never pull a knife unless you know how to use it."

The boy tensed and balled his hands into fists. Jaxon widened his stance and waited.

"Elias," the man scolded.

"Lesson two, kid, never take on an opponent unless you know you can win." Jaxon threw the knife at the kid making me gasp. It stuck in a tree no more than an inch over the boy's head. "You seem like a good group. A little rusty on manners, but it's been a rough night. Why don't we work together to find the tree we need to get out of here before the bad guys find us?"

The man—apparently the leader of this group—reluctantly agreed. The oldest of the women stayed with the young children, and the rest disappeared into the woods to search. Jaxon took my hand, keeping me close as we walked around each tree looking for a sign it was the one we needed. Although, how we were going to open up a doorway in a tree again was a mystery. Definitely going on the question list.

We searched tree after tree, but no sign of a lotus symbol.

Jaxon suggested that I try to reach out to the symbol

with my mind since I clearly had a connection. I thought he was crazy, but we couldn't spend all night in this forest. At first, nothing happened, then that sensation started like something unfurling inside me. I pictured the lotus symbol in my mind. My palms tingled, and I knew exactly where to go.

We all stood around the tree as I touched the metal lotus symbol once more. Several gasps rang out when the bluish-white light enveloped the trunk and the portal opened. People went through a couple at a time until Jaxon and I were the last ones left. He gripped my hand as we stepped up to the tree. My toes were brushing the edge of the portal when a hoarse voice bellowed from behind us, "Meara!"

We turned to find an elderly man in a dark suit staring at me as if he had seen a ghost. Beside him was the giant from earlier. His eyes were now a glacial blue, but flames were weaving around his knuckles as he watched us with a look of contempt. The gray-haired man stepped forward, his azure eyes locked on me.

"Meara, you came back to me," he choked out.

Before I could question who the man thought I was, Jaxon grabbed me by the waist and jumped though the portal.

14

We popped out of the same tree we had fallen through earlier and into the small clearing of the Emerald Rain Forest. We stumbled across the burn marks from the lightning strike, Jaxon's quick reflexes keeping us on our feet. His arms crushed me back against his chest like he was afraid someone would try to rip me away. Anger and fear warred across his face. "Are you ok?"

"I'm ok," I replied absentmindedly, still trying to make sense of everything that had happened. "You can let me go now."

"No, I really can't." His voice was rough and possessive. His lips brushed against my hair and his arms relaxed a bit. His voice was back to the playful Jaxon I knew when he said, "We have that talk coming, remember?"

A squeak of surprise escaped as I was pulled from Jaxon's arms. Lia wrapped me up in a bear hug almost suffocating me in her abundant cleavage. I hadn't noticed until now that the Kyrion and guides were all here as well. The guides surrounded the villagers, their hands out in a hostile gesture that said, 'One wrong move and you're toast.' I didn't know the people we had rescued, but I didn't think they were evil. They had been running for their lives the same as us.

"Can't. Breathe," I gasped.

Lia ignored my squirming. "Take shallow breaths. I'm not letting you go for at least a few hours."

"*Asteràki*, perhaps you could let your friend up for air at least to change into dry clothes while I deal with our ... guests." Bennett's deep voice of reason seemed to get through to her, and she gave me one final squeeze before letting me go. "The Kyrion must be apprised of what has happened. Meet us in the Order Hall in one hour."

Lia stayed right by my side as we made our way through the rain forest asking a dozen questions that I didn't have answers for. Eventually, she ran out of steam and silence descended over the group. The feeling of eyes on my back had my muscles tensing with every step we took, but I didn't want to set Lia off again by searching for the source.

We came to a stop in front of the elevators. A woman I think they had called Gaia, the Kyrion for the House of Seasons, walked toward the villagers. They watched her in awe. I couldn't blame them—she had an ethereal quality to her. Her dark blonde curls framed a face of angelic beauty. She seemed to float across the ground, her Grecian-style green dress not even moving as she walked. She addressed them in their language. The man I had identified as their leader doing most of the talking. Bennett and Jaxon broke away from the rest of Kyrion to talk in hushed tones. Lia was swatting at bugs. For the moment, no one was paying close attention to me.

I scanned over the crowd until my eyes collided with the faded brown eyes of the old woman from the village. A floral kerchief covered her head, two white braids trailed down to her knees. Her skin was a deep brown and lined with age, like leather when it had been well worn. Discs of metal and beads gleamed in the lantern light where they were woven into her braids and hanging around her neck. Her dress looked like a basket of sheets had been dumped over her and draped down to brush the tops of her bare feet.

She walked toward me saying something in her language, but "Meara" was the only thing I could understand. There was that name again.

I walked toward her, but Jaxon stepped between us. His taller form blocked my view. "Don't you have some random females to chase?"

"I seem to be chasing a feisty little brunette quite a bit lately. Trust me my hands are already full—or they could be if you moved a bit closer." I rolled my eyes and tried to step around him, but he blocked me again. "Until we know more about the villagers, you need to keep your distance."

"Jaxon, she's a little old lady. I think I've got this."

"Looks can be deceiving." He nodded his head to the side. "Remember the boy who held a knife on you only moments ago?"

I glanced over where the teenage boy they had called Elias was practically drooling over the food one of the servants was passing out. He took a huge bite from a chocolate bar, his face lighting up with so much bliss it was like he had seen Santa for the first time. He had been so tough in the woods near their village.

Dang it, Jaxon may have a point. Not that I was going to tell him that. "I want to know why she's been staring at me."

Jaxon crossed his arms. Those muscled arms that had wrapped around me ... *Uh, stop thinking about his arms!* I need to get the walking hormone factory out of the way, so I can try to talk to the old woman.

"Jaxon—" A yellow butterfly flitted between us. Then came back to circle around my head.

The rain forest had gone completely quiet.

Jaxon looked at me with a mixture of pride and concern before he stepped back to join the others who had gathered around us. More butterflies joined the first, some went to circle the old woman, some to circle around Gaia. They flew around the three of us, then met each other, then did it again. As if we all took orders from butterflies every day, the three of us met near the center of the small clearing.

"The butterflies on this island really love their welcoming parties." I tried to joke, but the women continued to watch the butterflies as if waiting. "Uh, does anyone have a clue what's going on?"

"Can you not hear them?" Gaia asked.

"Hear what?" The air grew thicker with butterflies until it looked like a snow globe of yellow separating us from the others.

"They are excited that you are here. They are calling you to join them, Chosen."

Gaia held out her finger and a butterfly landed. Her pale-green eyes were alight with what looked like excitement as she watched me carefully. If I hadn't been raised to give thanks to Mother Earth and to feel my connection with all of nature, this would probably be really strange. But I was so excited I was bouncing on my toes. Now that I thought about it, similar-looking butterflies had joined me on my rooftop hideaway often when I was young.

Was there some connection between that and what was happening now? Gaia had called me "Chosen." Did that mean that I had some special relationship with the butter-flies? More questions to add to my list.

"So how do I tune into their station?"

Gaia smiled at me like I was a favored pet. Then held her palm up toward me. She spoke briefly to the old woman before raising her other hand. The old woman placed her palm against Gaia's and held her other up toward me. The moment I completed the circle a current flowed from my palms up to my shoulders and down to my back where it felt like it traced a pattern onto my skin. Cold grew around me until our breath misted the air. My skin started to glow a faint bluish-white, and frost coated me. I tried to pull away, but they laced their fingers through mine and held on tightly.

"Your spirit power has been free to grow in strength," Gaia gritted out as frost crept along her hand to her wrist. "I sense the Spirit Kiss was bestowed long ago. Perhaps even when you were a babe. The spirit is using your power to fight us. It does not want to share you with the Goddess."

I couldn't say anything—even if I knew how to respond to that mix of information. At the moment I was too cold to even shiver. If I died of hypothermia in the middle of a rain forest, I wanted my name in the *Guinness Book of World Records*.

The old woman said something, then tugged me toward her using our linked hands. It was awkward being chest to chest with this woman with my hands still clasped. I stared down into her craggy face. Her eyes held a well of sadness that caused my throat to tighten. A single tear fell and froze to my cheek. She nodded to me. Although I was sure I wouldn't understand a word of what she said, I leaned down. Pressure built in my ears as she sang a beautiful song in one ear and then into the other. I winced as the pressure grew until my ears popped.

"Meara, I feel your presence in her. The wrongs done you, they are ours, not hers. We loved you and thought we knew what was best." Pain choked her voice as tears slipped down the old woman's cheeks. "You must let the Goddess claim her. She is strong, there is room for you both."

I didn't know how I was now able to understand her, but her words only seemed to make things worse. The frost bit into my skin and spilled down the old woman's arm. She gasped in pain. I wanted to help her, but I didn't know how to help any of us. My frustration grew, and a new energy filled me. I lifted one foot at a time, stomping them to the ground and shattering the thickening frost. But it re-formed just as quickly. Both women were now gasping in the cold, and the frost had made it all the way to their shoulders. I needed to break our hold before they were injured.

I gathered my strength and propelled myself backward as hard as I could. I managed a couple of stumbling steps, but we were locked together too tightly.

The frost was climbing up their necks when I noticed movement out of the corner of my eye. The butterflies were changing formation. A group had broken off from the circling mass and were heading toward us. They dived at me like kamikaze fighters. Instead of bouncing off like I would have expected, they sank down into the layer of frost as though they were being preserved in sap. I was covered by an icy blanket of yellow butterflies.

Crack. Crack. Crack.

The noise sounded deafening in our frozen circle. Suddenly, the frost shattered. I fell to the ground, damp and shivering. Strong hands pulled me against a solid chest, and I shook even harder as Jaxon's warmth met my cold skin.

Blankets appeared out of thin air, and he wrapped us up in layers there on the wet ground.

"You know the best way to get warm is skin to skin," he whispered against the top of my head.

"N-n-not h-h-happening."

The old woman leaned over us and poked Jaxon with a stick. "Boy, move and let the Goddess do her work."

He responded in the same language, "Elder, she has been cold for too long, and I fear for her health."

"The Goddess takes care of her own or have you forgotten the old ways?" The woman poked him again. "Have the great House leaders fallen so far as to deny the power of our gods?"

"Elder ..."

"My name is Rosella," she replied imperiously.

"Elder Rosella, I mean no offense—"

"You do offend, boy! Now release my granddaughter before I show you the error of your ways."

"G-Granddaughter?" I whispered incredulously. "First, a man wearing a s-suit in the middle of nowhere—that just screams evil v-villain, by the way—thinks I'm s-someone he knows. Then I get f-frozen because I'm apparently lugging around some spirit b-baggage. Those poor butterflies *died* to keep me from becoming a Dia-cicle. Now a Rom elder thinks I'm her granddaughter. Curiouser and curiouser."

"Remember when I told you there were things you needed to know?" Jaxon brushed the hair back from my face and placed a kiss on my forehead. "This isn't how I wanted to have this conversation, but too much has happened. You are one of us—a Paldimori. You don't know what that means yet, but you are very special. If the stick gouging my shoulder is any indication, I believe we may have also found some of your family. Ouch! Damnit, ok, I'm getting up."

Jaxon got to his feet rubbing his shoulder but stayed close. Rosella made me get rid of the blanket and lie down on the wet grass. The silence was broken only by the chattering of my teeth. The air around me seemed to grow thicker pressing me down into the muddy grass. An itch popped up at the base of my spine, and I wriggled to scratch it. The tingling grew worse like thousands of ants marching along my back.

Then the ground moved beneath me. Roots shot up from the ground to wrap around my wrists and ankles. A sweet scent filled the air. Something soft grazed my hip. I felt the same sensation all around me. The roots pushed me upward until I hung in their grasp feet off the ground. A circle of yellow lotus flowers made the perfect outline of my body on the ground below where the shards of iced butterflies had dissolved. The wind picked up, carrying leaves that stuck to my naked body. Then the yellow lotus petals were ripped up by the wind. Together they molded into an elaborate dress.

I was dry, warm, and dressed like a fairy queen. The crowd below me stared open-mouthed, just as stunned as I. Except Lia, her hands were on her hips, and she looked two seconds from finding an ax to chop me down.

This is amazing! Why is she so angry?

The roots speared through my wrists. I screamed, and the wind rose with a shriek of fury to rip at the roots that I could swear were wriggling through my veins. Blood splashed the yellow petals of my full skirt and pain knifed along my back like the skin was being ripped away. My vision expanded.

I saw the village we had transported to through the portal, the land around it laid to waste.

Then I was underwater staring at the remains of a city and the crumbled landscape.

One scene after another of devastation and pain overwhelmed my senses.

A voice whispered in my head, "*Rest, my child.*"

I gave myself over to the soothing balm of that voice and knew no more.

15

The sun beamed down on the meadow in the training area where I waited for Molly to show me what we were doing today. My thoughts were a jumble of questions and more questions as I absently twirled a purple flower between my fingers. I'd woken up in my rooms this morning to find Molly yelling at a furious Jaxon. It had taken a moment to recognize him because the transition had been so dramatic.

His hair was in a disheveled mess around his face. His eyes were pitch black as they met mine across the room, the emotions pouring from them hitting me like a thunderclap. His clothes were wrinkled and torn as if he'd been in a fight. Molly had her hands pressed against his chest pushing him back through the doorway to my bedroom. The last thing I saw before unconsciousness claimed me again was him breaking away from her and reaching his hand out for me.

When I'd finally woken for good, Molly's cousin had been sitting on the edge of my bed humming. She had let me know that the Kyrion had taken away the villagers to some unknown location and called a meeting to discuss what happened. Molly and Lia had been required to attend as well. I'd asked her a dozen questions, but she hadn't known the answers. I hoped Molly would have some when she got out of the meeting.

I secretly hoped that Jaxon would come as well. His actions when he'd seen me this morning didn't seem like a man who only had sex on his mind. What was happening between us? Had he felt that zing when our eyes met? Those were just more questions to add to the list.

Finally, Molly joined me. My questions hit her rapid-fire. She cut me off and told me to pick two. I went with the most important. "Is my grandmother ok?"

"She's fine. She's giving everyone hell." Molly gave me a mischievous smile that was more like the woman I had been told about. "She's great."

My breath whooshed out in relief. *Thank you, Great Mother!* "What about what happened last night. That can't be normal, right? I mean, I believe in Mother Earth and talk to flowers, but I've never had plants try to turn me into a pin cushion. Not that—"

Molly held up her hands in a time out gesture. "I'll tell you what I know. Then you have to stop talking. Seriously, I thought only my cousin talked this much." She huffed, then turned on her heel and started walking away. "Keep up. I don't want to listen to Jaxon bitch if anything else happens to you. Consider us attached at the hip until further notice."

We walked toward the stream that ran through the middle of the meadow, and Molly stooped to pull a sack from a hollowed-out stump. "The Paldimori are descendants of six gods and goddesses. Your history books would call them the primordial gods. Everything was going great, then the Chaonian War happened. The descendants fought against each other and a lot of our people died. Some got away and ended up here in Sotirìa. Some got lost in the human world." Molly handed me an apple then glared at me when I took a bite. She grabbed another from the sack and put it in my other hand. Then grabbed my wrist and dragged me over to a gray-and-white Appaloosa. She shoved our hands at the horse. I giggled as it closed its mouth around the apple and our hands. Molly even cracked a tiny smile before getting back to business. "You've seen the cards. They've got some power in them to identify anyone with Paldimori blood. The problem is, they can't judge how much power people like you have."

She patted the horse and wiped her hand off on her pants. "Each House has a primary set of powers. Not everyone gets all of the powers or the same strength." She pinched her fingers together, then pulled them apart about three inches. "That's the size of most of the House symbols you'll see people marked with. The bigger the symbol, the more power someone has. Everyone I've ever seen come from the human world, their powers were repressed. The Games were designed to draw out the contestants' powers. Or, at least, we thought that was all they were for."

Molly's fingers drummed against her thigh as she squinted at the stream. "Jaxon and Lia have found some books in her father's library. Seems like her mom and dad were collecting info on the Chosen. The Games may have been set up to draw them out. The guides aren't the trusted advisors we once were. So, I'm only guessing here, but I think what happened last night was the Chosen version of having your powers awoken."

"Gaia called me 'Chosen' too. What does that mean?"

"That's another question." Molly ran her hand over her

face in irritation. "Fine, I'll answer this last one. You went through a lot yesterday and aren't crying about it. Not everyone will have their powers awoken when they come here. Those that don't go back to the human world none the wiser. The last few years there have been fewer and fewer awakenings. Everyone is worried. Our communities are being attacked, you saw it when you were in Chaméni Elpída."

"Wait, what's that? Cami ...?"

"Kah-men-yay El-peeda," she sounded out. "It's the name of the village where you found your grandmother.

"Our enemies don't care who they kill. Their goal is to wipe us out. The attacks have been getting worse. But it isn't just that." Molly's hands fisted, a look of bitter disappointment tightened her features. "More of our children are born with weaker powers. Fewer new people are added through the Games. We're a dying race, Dia."

Silence stretched between us. These poor people. They were being persecuted for simply being who they were. My heart ached for them. I knew exactly how that felt.

"Enough about that." Molly picked out another apple. "C'mon its time you met Saam."

She stepped up onto the hollowed-out tree trunk and whistled. A reddish-brown horse on the other side of the stream lifted its head and whinnied. It walked through the stream and stopped in front of Molly.

I finished the apple I was eating and walked over to join them. "Wow, he's beautiful."

Molly snorted. "Don't let him fool you. Saam is his nickname. His real name is Stubborn as a Mule."

"You want me to ride a horse you named 'Stubborn as a Mule?'"

"He's the fastest," Molly said, while keeping the apple away from the horse. "The triathlon is all about speed. Trust me you'll want Saam. After the swim, you're going to be tired. You'll have some time to recharge for the race at the end."

"Can't I ride a bicycle like normal people do in those races? I know where the brakes are, and it won't bite me."

"No. And Saam doesn't bite." Molly tossed me the apple. I held it out to the horse as he turned toward me. As if to disprove her, Saam chomped down especially hard on the apple. I checked my fingers to make sure they were all still there.

"Let me get this straight. I have to swim, ride a horse, and then race on foot. All in one day?"

"Yep." Saam nudged Molly's shoulder, and a sad little smile slipped across her face. She rubbed his neck, and he leaned into her touch like an affectionate child. "Oof. I'm rationing your apples. Don't look at me like that. You're going to be too fat to win. Do you want me to put Ninny in the competition instead?"

He snorted as if to say, "Yeah, right." The gray-and-white Appaloosa from earlier looked up when she heard her name. She wrinkled up her nose exposing big white teeth in the goofiest horse smile I'd ever seen. Saam tossed his head and stomped his foot.

"Ok, ok. Point taken," Molly surrendered with a smile that seemed less forced. "I'll keep you in. No showing off. Just get to the front and stay there."

I'm pretty sure the horse would have saluted if he could have. Instead, he did a weird bowing thing before he trotted off after Ninny who was distracted with smelling all the flowers. Molly kneeled down at the stream to splash water on her face. A laugh burst out before I could stop it when Saam circled back to steal an apple from the bag sitting behind her.

She stood and dried off her face with the hem of her red tank top. "He took an apple, didn't he?"

"Huh-hum," I pretended to clear my throat to try to cover up my laugh. "So what else can you tell me about the competition?" No way was I going to make the horse who was supposed to carry me through part of this competition mad at me. I pulled a small box of Nerds out of the pocket of my yoga pants and enjoyed a snack.

"How can you eat that crap? Saam, I see you. No more apples." Molly dropped to the ground with a sigh. "I'm too tired to deal with mutiny. I'll work it out of you both tomorrow."

I groaned. "My muscles are crying for mercy already."

"Should have thought of that before you sided with the horse."

"We're bonding for the competition."

"Your ass. His back. That's all the 'bonding' you need." She glanced at me over her shoulder, a bitter note entering her voice. "You're a Chosen, shouldn't be that hard."

"Why do you hate me?" I asked. "I mean we don't have to be besties, but you act like I kicked your cat. I would never kick a cat, by the way. I love cats. Horses are going to take some time, but I'm sure I'll love them too."

"That's a record." Molly gave me a weak little grin. "Thought you'd keep going 'til time for the race."

My running monologue could last a while, especially when I was excited about something. It was like releasing the pressure from a corked bottle and letting out all of the randomness going on in my head. It was a relief for me, but not so much for everyone else. Surprisingly, my head was quieter than usual today. All of my life I had been looking for a way to drown out the constant chatter. Now that I had a little peace, it felt strange. Almost like a part of me was missing.

"I don't hate you," Molly said quietly, her gaze direct and honest. "You have Jaxon all confused, which is reason enough to like you. You're nice. Funny. Sweet, even, but not to the point of gagging me. We could have been friends before ..."

"Before what?" She turned away, refusing to answer. "What about Lia? I thought you were close. She told me she wants—"

"No!" Molly jumped to her feet, her hands clenching at her sides as she faced me. Tears filled her eyes, and she roughly swiped them away. "The last Chosen I got involved with cost me more than I can bear. Don't talk to me about her. I'll teach you and train you. That's my job. But that's all I can give you."

"I'm sorry for whatever happened to you," I said softly, really wishing I could give her a hug.

She nodded. "You asked about the competition. I'll tell you what I can." She settled back onto the ground and picked up a blade of grass to wrap around her finger. "Pétra Skiá Kástro —Stone Shadow Castle—is your end goal. It was the home of the House of Shadows when our ancestors lived here full-time."

I squinted against the sunlight that somehow filled the cave where the training area was located and pulled a tress of my hair over my shoulder. My hands worked absently braiding my hair as Molly continued her story. Sotiría was created as a sanctuary for the surviving Paldimori people when their society collapsed. The Houses were created as forms of government to help protect the six family lines. One person for each house would rule and assume the title of the original founder of the lines. Eventually, a decision was made by the rulers to spread the Houses around the world and create territories for each that they would rule over.

"You've seen the powers we have. Hell, you and Lia are the most powerful among us. The Chosen." Molly stood and walked to the water's edge. She bent to pick up a rock and sent it skipping across the stream.

"There's a prophecy about the Chosen. Only a few of our people remember it. And no one knows who told it. When I was little, my birth mother would tell me stories about the Chosen. She was the Kafàli for my line. They get a bit more info than us normal guides." Molly threw another rock. "I was supposed to follow in her footsteps. Instead, I was a disappointment."

She squeezed the rock in her hand so hard, it looked like it would crack. "And Grace said something about the Chosen saving us or dooming us. I'd never heard that last part. Damn it, now they're both dead. Whatever they knew is gone."

Molly threw the rock so hard it sailed right over the creek and hit Ninny in the rump. The horse jumped and let out a whinny. Then turned narrowed eyes our way and bit at the air. "Fuck!" Molly slammed her fist against her thigh. "Sorry, girl. How about another apple?"

A yellow apple floated out of the bag and over to the horse. She stared at us a few minutes before she accepted the peace offering and gobbled it up. Molly wrapped her arms around herself and hung her head.

"It was an accident," I assured her as I got to my feet. "Ninny's ok."

"She's fine now, but what about next time? What if that had been a kid?' Molly said more to herself than me and tightened her grip until her knuckles creaked. "I'm so angry all the time. Guides can't be unstable. We can't lose control. I don't know how to be anything but a guide. It's the one thing I'm good at."

"Hey, no one's going to make you give up your job." I put my hand on her shoulder. She tensed but didn't knock me on my butt. "You're grieving, and you need time to deal with what happened. I'm sure your boss can understand that. I know what it's like to be angry at the universe for taking people from you. You'll find a way to handle it. Me, I started self-defense classes. They helped me to put the anger to good use."

I stepped back grateful she hadn't punched me. "If you want to talk sometime, you know where to find me."

"You ..." Molly cleared her throat and turned to face me. Her smoky blue-gray eyes were large and haunted. "Why are you being nice to me? I've been a bitch to you since we met."

"I can't stand to see people or animals hurting. Lia calls it my savior complex, but if I can help, why wouldn't I?" I shrugged "Besides it takes too much energy to stay mad. But there may be a few exceptions to that rule."

"Jaxon," we said together and laughed.

"Thanks, Dia. I-I don't think I'm ready to talk about it. But when I am, I'll come find you."

"I hope you do. I think we could be friends. And, you know, Lia loves you." I held up my hand when her face darkened. "She does, and she's not giving up on your friendship either."

"Enough Kumbaya"—she made a gagging face—"It's time to get to work. Sorry about this."

I frowned. "Sorry? About wh—"

She waved her hand, and a bubble of water about the size of a beach ball lifted into the air. It flew straight into my chest, and I shrieked as icy cold water soaked me.

Molly grinned. "Now you're ready to ride."

16

A soft breeze rustled through the leaves of the forest and tugged gently at my braid. I inhaled deeply, taking in the sweet scent of the purple flowers in the meadow mixed with the almost lemony tang of the grasses. I popped another almond in my mouth, relishing the cherry-vanilla hints. Molly had complained that I was a bottomless pit as she withdrew the bag of almonds from the miracle stump and tossed them to me when my belly wouldn't stop rumbling. Usually I would have had a bag full of snacks, but I hadn't exactly had time to raid the kitchen with everything going on.

I stood and stretched. My butt and legs protested every move. Molly hadn't been kidding about Saam's speed. She'd started us off at a walk around the meadow, but Saam didn't have much patience for that. He'd taken off like a bullet, and I'd barely been able to hang on. The ride had been made even more difficult by my wet clothes. Soggy spandex, the bare back of a horse, and breakneck speeds wasn't a combination I would recommend. But my initial terror had calmed after a bit, and I'd been able to feel a connection to

Saam. We'd worked well together as a team after that, and I'd found a new love for horseback riding.

I tipped my head back to soak in the artificial sunlight of the cave. This is what life should be like. My head was calm. My blood was pumping after practicing with Saam. My senses were tingling with a newfound sensation as though I was connected to everything around me. I plucked another almond from the drawstring bag and tossed it in my mouth. A rough shove from behind caused me to stumble and the almond lodged in my throat. I bent over coughing. Tears streamed down my face as I wheezed and struggled to dislodge the nut.

A kick landed to the back of my knee sending me to the ground.

I rolled with the fall and back onto my feet like I'd been taught. I wheezed around the almond and shakily took a fighter stance as my teary eyes scanned the area for my attacker. All I saw was a shadow disappearing into the woods. No one else was around. I dropped my hands and tried coughing out the almond. My throat worked convulsively to trying to dislodge it, but it wasn't working. I stuck my fingers in my mouth hoping I could reach it.

Then the weirdest thing happened. My fingertips tingled, and there was a tugging sensation along my back. My eyes widened in horror as something slithered down my throat. I yanked my fingers out and gasped a full breath. Waving from the tip of my finger was a small green sprout. Its two leaves opened to show me the almond that I had been choking on.

Lia and Bennett appeared a few feet in front of me. Literally appeared out of thin air. My best friend had some explaining to do. She was clearly more in the know about this place than she had let on. I wasn't as dumb as most people thought. I understood that Lia must have been Paldimori too since she had gotten into the Games the same way I had. Why hadn't she told me what it meant when I activated the card? Anger and hurt sat like a boulder on my chest.

"I've been so worried about you," I stood stiffly in her arms as Lia hugged me. "Dumbass Jaxon scooped you up before I could get to you last night. Then the caveman behind me refused to let me near the training area until you took a break." She pulled back and cocked her head as she noticed my finger. "Why is there a plant growing out of your finger?"

I wanted to shout at her and demand to know everything she had been withholding. But the other contestants were gathering for the start of the race. We would be talking later though, whether she wanted to or not. I took a deep breath and pushed it all away to deal with later.

I filled her in on what happened. Lia stomped around cussing and threatening anatomically impossible acts on whoever had attacked me. Bennett stood back smiling as she threatened him and Jaxon as well. My focus never wavered from the sprout. I ran a finger along the line where my skin merged with the green base. The shoot dropped the almond in my palm and slowly sank back into my skin.

How amazing would it be if I could grow anything with a single thought? I imagined an orange tiger lily. A small perfect flower grew out of my forearm. I bounced up and down, throwing my hands out to see if I could get more flowers to grow.

Squeee, new way to decorate my clothes!

I'd heard about people who knew exactly where to plant the best crops and whose flowers bloomed all year round. But nothing like this. On her good days, Mom had been clear-headed enough to tell me about the things people in her tribe could do. She'd said that we were blessed by the Great Mother to share a connection with all of nature that let us be able to work together. I'd loved those stories but had written them off as something she made up as part of her sickness.

I wished she were here to see me now.

Tiger lilies started popping up around my feet. Bennett was giving me a knowing look.

The same look Lia gave me as she plucked a flower from the ground. I knew what they were thinking, but they were wrong. I didn't make tiger lilies because I was thinking of Jaxon. Nope. He hadn't even crossed my mind. Except when I woke up in his shirt this morning. Maybe when Molly and I were talking his name came up. *Dang it, ok, so maybe I can't stop thinking about him.* It's his fault for being all super-model-y perfection that makes my girl parts sweat.

"You have so much more control than I do already," Lia said in awe, breaking into my Jaxon-filled thoughts.

The giddy happiness that had filled me vanished. She'd finally admitted she had powers too. "Why didn't you tell me?"

"I wanted to." She stuffed her hands in her pockets. "I know I promised not to keep more secrets from you. But I swore an oath to the Kyrion, just like you did. I should have told you no matter what. I knew that you had to be part-Paldimori since you had activated the card before. But I didn't know about the different messages until a few days ago."

The guilty look she gave me confirmed that they knew I was Chosen when I had activated my card. "The cards usually only show an invitation, but ours had that message about being chosen and finding what you seek. You were woken by Gaia, just as I was woken by Chaos. We think the card really is identifying the Chosen, but we still don't know what the rest of the message means. I had hoped that we were wrong. That you wouldn't have to go through the pain of being connected to a god like I was."

Lia was gripping her hands together so tightly they were turning white. "I don't expect you to forgive me again. You don't deserve the hell I've put you through. Any of it." Tears slipped silently down her cheeks, her face a grim mask of regret. "You should have been safe here. I never thought they would come after you or I would have tried harder to keep you from coming here. This is all my fault. I'm so sorry, Dia."

Bennett wrapped his arms around her and pulled her back against his chest. "*Asteràki*, the fault is no one's but those who wish to harm the Chosen. Do not take on this guilt. If you must blame someone, then blame me. I am ruler here. Yet, once again, a Potential under my care was attacked."

"Damnit, Bennett, I let her come here," Lia growled. "I didn't tell her about being Paldimori or that we have enemies that would try to kill her just for being what she is. This isn't on you. You can't protect us all every second of every day."

"Ok, then, everyone is guilty. Yay, we'll throw a party." I said sarcastically. "In the meantime, can someone explain to me what just happened?" I waved my hands to indicate all of the flowers. "Did you see that? Please tell me random plants aren't going to be growing out of me. I'm picturing a total *Aliens* moment."

"Calm down, sweetie. Nothing is going to grow out of you that you don't want to." Lia turned to Bennett. "Uh, right?"

"Yes. Dia, you were claimed by Gaia. The goddess of Earth. I believe your grandmother called her the Great Mother. Others call her Mother Earth." Bennett nodded toward the flowers. "The plants. Trees. The land. Animals. Water. They all answer your call now. You have powers gifted by Gaia herself. Much like Lia was claimed by Chaos and received her powers from him."

"Yeah, that wasn't an experience that I would wish on anyone." Lia shuddered. "Apparently the gods think that claiming their Chosen has to be served with a side of epic pain. Someone should clue them in to the twenty-first century. Maybe try laser tattooing instead of crawling inside us and burning their brand on our backs like cows."

"I had a goddess inside me?" I rubbed at my wrists where the roots had dug themselves into my veins. "Guess that's one way to be one with Mother Nature. What brand?"

"You haven't seen it yet?" Lia paused and turned in Bennett's arms. She laid her hands on his bare pecs and roughly rubbed them. "C'mon, wizard, we need a mirror."

Bennett growled at her, "Woman, I am not a wizard, nor a genie."

"All-powerful Chaos descendant, I wish for a mirror. Does that help?"

"I prefer you call me 'my god' like you did—"

"Uh, thanks," I interrupted. "I think we all get the kind of rubbing you want her to do. But can we maybe focus on me being possessed for a minute?"

A stand mirror appeared next to me, and I did a double take. Uh huh, not a wizard or a genie? I was with Lia on this one.

Lia walked me over to the mirror. She nudged me until I turned around. and then lifted my shirt up to expose my back. Her fingers traced a pattern across my back, and I glanced over my shoulder. Like the branding iron Lia had talked about, there were lines of pale pink skin in the shape of a tree. The roots sank down below the waist of my pants, and gnarled limbs reached across my shoulder blades.

"It's just like mine was after that night in the courtyard. Before our bond," Lia said to Bennett.

My heart was threatening to beat right out of my chest. "What is it? What does it mean?"

"This is the beginning of Gaia's mark. It means you will be very powerful." Bennett placed his hand on my shoulder and looked me in the eye. "It also means you are in danger. The Paldimori are hunted. You saw this yourself at Chaméni Elpída."

"Those GI Joe people that were attacking the villagers want to kill me?" I asked. Then it registered what he said. "Oh god—er, goddess—we're in so much trouble. Have you seen those guys? Riiiight. Well, it's been fun. How about you call me a plane? I'll go back to Normalville and leave you to your games. I'm a lover, not a fighter."

Lia dropped my shirt into place and nudged Bennett out of the way. "I wish we could. But this is kinda like Hotel California. Your powers have been awakened. You can't put them back in the box." She gave me a sad little smile. "Trust me. I left here, and the bad guys found me anyway. You remember the boiler explosion at my parents' house? That isn't what really happened. Natalie is Paldimori as well. She used her wind power to knock me into a support column, and I almost died. You were there. You saw it. She—"

"What?" The bottom dropped out of my stomach. Dread sat like a knife aimed at my heart. That image I'd shrugged off of Lia flying through the air as wind whipped around us came back. "If there wasn't an explosion why do I remember your parents' house being wrecked? Why do I remember you having burn marks when I visited you in the hospital?"

"Your memories were altered," she whispered. Her shoulders slumped, and she refused to meet my eyes. Shocked disbelief swept through me like a hurricane. Then pain at her betrayal cut me so deep I thought I was bleeding out. "We hadn't figured out then that you were Paldimori. They ... We couldn't risk you knowing about us. That's how the Paldimori have stayed hidden all this time."

The knife twisted deeper at her mention of "us". Like they were her family, not me—not the one person who had stuck by her side no matter what all these years.

"Anyone who learns too much get their memories altered." Lia finally met my gaze, her eyes pleaded with me to understand. "Even the Potentials who get sent home. I didn't put the pieces together about you being able to see the invite until Jaxon mentioned that he thought he felt something when you first met and wanted to test it out on you. I'm sorry, Dia. I wanted to tell you everything—"

"Did you? Or was this one more thing you thought stupid, naive Dia couldn't handle? One more thing that poor little damaged Lia had to face on her own?" I backed away, feeling sick to my stomach. Lia let out an agonized whimper, but I ignored it. What kind of person let others scramble your brain, then helped them continue the lies? Had she ever cared about me? All she had done was take without giving back. My hands shook as the anger feed my power. Dirt erupted in a shower a few feet in front of me. Then again. A stag sprang from the forest. His massive antlers lowered in challenge as he charged toward Lia. He stopped with his horns only inches from her and snorted threateningly.

"Dia, please." She tried to get around the stag, but he

blocked her every move. "Please call off the deer and let me explain."

"You don't get to act like the victim here," I said. My voice sounded unnatural even to my own ears—like all emotion had been stripped away. "I've stood by you through everything. I searched for you when you disappeared without a word. I welcomed you back with open arms when you popped back into my life and never pushed you for answers. I've smiled every time you ripped me to pieces by pushing me away. This ... You mistrusted me so much you took my memories from me?"

"No, it wasn't like that." Lia cried out, reaching for me. "I didn't—"

"Save it!" I shouted. "I don't want to hear any more. You aren't the person I thought you were. I guess *she* really did die with her parents."

Lia gasped and clutched her chest like I had stabbed her. For a moment, guilt tried to edge out my pain, and I regretted my cruel words. There was a part of me that wanted to hug her and tell her we could work this out too. But this wasn't her being distant or trying to protect me. This time she was the one who put me in danger by not telling me the truth. My chest caved in. Dan had stolen what confidence I'd built for myself. Lia did so much more. She smashed my belief in the goodness of people and the conviction that family are the people who will stand with you against the world.

"You can go now," I said coldly. "I have training to do."

"D-Dia, please," Lia pleaded, reaching for me again.

"Go!"

Lia let out a heartbroken sob.

Bennett's hard eyes assessed me. A muscle worked in his

rugged jaw. "I hope you know what you are doing. Traveling a road alone is more difficult than you think."

"I've been alone a long time."

"You have never been as alone as you will be if you choose this path." The thinning of his lips and the hard glint in his eyes said he was speaking from experience. "Things are not always what they seem when glimpsed through the eyes of pain. Why not rest and discuss this further tomorrow?"

"I'm not a child! And I'm done being a doormat for everyone."

"Cutting yourself off from those you love can leave wounds that run too deep to ever be healed. I ask you not to do this."

"Should I just keep letting everyone take their stab at me until I bleed to death?" The stag pawed the ground, ready to charge at my slightest signal. "It's time I stood up for myself and stopped being so damn nice."

"So be it," Bennett said ominously. "Since you no longer want Lia here, I am taking her away."

He scooped a sobbing Lia up in his arms and they vanished.

17

The lingering anger I still felt the next day helped me push through all of my exercises in record time. I was finishing up on the weight bench now, a concerned-looking Jaxon hovering by my side. The sound of the other contestants working out filled the otherwise silent gym. Everyone had been giving me space since yesterday, probably afraid I would send my new friend after them if they got on my nerves. The stag had waited patiently while we finished the race, then tried to follow me to my rooms. I'd had no clue how get him to go back to wherever he came from. Luckily, Gaia helped me figure it out.

"Where's Molly?" I asked.

"She had errands." Jaxon helped me rack the bar, and I sat up on the weight bench dabbing a towel at my sweaty neck. "You don't have a problem with me being your trainer today, do you, Tigerlily?"

"Nope." I hopped off the bench and quickly skirted around him. "Did you send her on these 'errands' on purpose?"

"Maybe." Jaxon followed me to the mats at the back of

the gym area. "Is there a reason you're always running away from me?"

"I'm not running. I'm concentrating." My feet planted on the mat, I straightened my whole body getting into the Mountain Pose. "Tada ... saaana. Tada ... saaana."

"Are you chanting?"

"Yes, it's a prayer to get rid of pesky playboys." I stretched my arms up toward the ceiling. It probably wasn't a good idea to do a forward bend with Jaxon so near, but I couldn't bring myself to care that he was staring. I wouldn't tell him this, but his being here was helping me keep it together. For some reason, I found his presence comforting, and it scared me. "Why are you here? I've already gone through all of the exercises we've been doing."

"Oh, I'm just here for the view. What else?" he said with a bite to his voice. He sighed and ran a hand through his hair. "I'm sorry. You've had a rough couple of days and don't need me making it worse. How're you doing?"

My throat closed on the words that wanted to spill out in a torrent of grief and pain. Why did I want to pour out my soul to this man? Hadn't I had enough betrayals lately?

"I'm fine."

Silence stretched out for a few minutes. I looked up to find Jaxon staring at me as if he was torn about what to say. I could tell the moment he made his decision. His eyes darkened to nearly black and his shoulders went rigid. "I don't think you are."

"I don't want to talk about it." I straightened from my position to glare at him.

"Funny thing, it seems you don't want to talk to anyone about quite a few things." Grim determination tightened his face. "I understand your fear about your memories being altered. You wonder what else could have been altered.

Then you start to question everything. Eventually, you don't know who or what you can trust."

I sucked in a hard breath as he voiced every thought that had kept me pacing the floors most of the night. "How did you—"

"I'm the one who altered your memories," he blurted out. His face was carefully blank, but his eyes raged with emotions.

"Wh—What?"

"Lia was dying, again. You were a hysterical mess." His hands fisted, and a grimace crossed his face as if it was a memory that he would've changed as well. "I made the decision to alter your memories. I used Voice—it's like a compulsion—to keep you calm until Erebus could come wipe your mind. I came up with the boiler explosion story to replace what had happened and he weaved them into new memories."

His eyes were locked with mine when he said, "This was not Lia's doing."

Maybe it wasn't, but she'd still helped them lie. "You ... Why do you care?"

"You deserve to know the whole truth, even if that means you'll hate me for it."

I laughed bitterly. The sound was harsh and painful to hear, like fingernails on a chalkboard. He flinched but didn't look away. "I must be the biggest idiot in the world. Why do I keep trusting people who betray me?"

He looked surprised that I said I had trusted him. I trusted the man I could see beneath the surface. The one that was smart and kind. That was the man that I had started to fall for. Not the playboy mask he showed to the world.

The quietness of the gym finally registered, and I turned to give our audience a "mind your own business" look.

Jaxon lifted his hand and what little sound there had been died away. "I've put us in a sort of bubble. No one can hear or see us. You aren't a show for their entertainment."

I swallowed thickly, but I wouldn't let his thoughtfulness derail me.

"You had no right to mess with my head. Did you know that my mother suffered from depression? No, you didn't, because you don't know anything about me. You don't know that seeing the only family I had fight demons I couldn't see tied me up in knots and caused anxiety attacks. You didn't know that I have questioned my own mental health every single day of my life, so afraid that I would end up just like her."

His face went pale. His mouth opened but nothing came out. The colorful scraps of fabric he had been holding fell to the mat.

"I don't wear black, ever." I waved my hand at the lime green and peach yoga outfit I was wearing. "Because that is the color of my childhood. The windows were always covered, and the lights kept off when it got really bad. My mother wore the same black dress for days on end, only showering when I forced her to. I became the opposite of everything I hated."

My hands fisted as an echo of the cruel words from my youth filled my mind. "I know that I'm not normal. That normal people don't hear all of these different voices in their heads. But as long as I could still laugh, I was ok, and I've learned to deal with my quirks." I sighed, suddenly so very tired. "You've made me question everything I thought I knew about myself."

Jaxon's hand gripped mine and wouldn't let go. "I'm so

very sorry, Dia. For what you went through as a child, and what I've done to you. You're right, I didn't know anything about you. I didn't even think about what effect my decision would have on you; I was trying to protect my people."

He had protected his people at my expense, for his greater good. I might have been able to respect that, but I was too raw. I hadn't been able to stem the bleeding from the wounds already inflicted before being stabbed again.

His other hand came up to cup my cheek, and I flinched. He dropped his hand, his eyes pools of despair that I refused to acknowledge. "You aren't your mother. You're like the sunshine—so bright and beautiful that you draw people to you. Yes, you're complicated, but that isn't a bad thing. Don't let my bad decision make you doubt yourself. I know all too well what that's like. I've questioned who I am my whole life."

My body reacted to his nearness, his touch like the missing piece of a puzzle I didn't even know was unfinished. But my head was screaming not to be a fool again. I pulled away from him and wrapped my arms around my waist. "Why would you question yourself? You're a famous model who can have any woman in the world, right? Or are you the hard-nosed lawyer? Wait, maybe you're the sweet guy who slips out every now and then? When you take off the playboy mask, who are you really, Jaxon?"

"I-I don't know." There was a vulnerability about him in this moment that I had never seen before. "My memories were altered too."

He stared off over my shoulder, his body held so much tension he was like a guitar string pulled too tight. "My family estate was attacked like the village of Chaméni Elpída. I was three and Nat was five. We were the only survivors." His voice faltered for a moment before he cleared his throat and continued. "Because I was so young, it was decided to remove all of my memories. Sometimes I wonder what my family was like. I wonder if I look like my mother or my father. I've spent years trying to fill in those gaps with research and chasing down leads. I'm good at it. That's why I became a lawyer. I always want the truth, even when it hurts. We're alike in that regard."

My chest ached for the little boy who had lost everything. We had more in common than I ever thought possible. I wanted to be able to reach out to him, but I was scared. Every time I reached out, I got slapped back down by some new betrayal. Everything lately seemed to be boiling down to fear. Fear of what I would discover here about myself. Fear of these powers that I could feel building inside me. Fear for my newfound family that I had yet to be able to talk to. Fear that Lia and I really were permanently broken this time. Fear of what I still felt for this man even after his confession.

"I'm sorry about your family," I whispered. "Thank you for telling me, but that doesn't change what you did to me. You, of all people, should hate what you are doing to people."

He nodded. "I'll ask Molly to come back to finish out the day with you. I really am sorry, Dia."

The sounds of the gym rushed back in as he dropped the barrier and walked away. I ignored the pang in my heart that didn't want him to go. I had made the right decision. I was going to win these Games and find a teaching job where I could make a new start. Mom had been talking about traveling lately: she would love us exploring a new place together. My mom and Mr. Skittles were all I needed.

"Hi, uh, what was your name again?" A silky voice interrupted my thoughts.

I turned to find Nikki, her blue eyes darting between Jaxon's retreating form and me. "Dia," I replied. "You're Nikki, right?"

"That's me," she giggled and held out a goblet to me. "Here, I thought you might be thirsty. I know I am. They work us like slaves. I don't think I've ever sweated so much in my life."

I took the surprisingly heavy metal cup. I'd been working out non-stop for over an hour. I tipped the cup, taking long sips to cool my thirst. "Thanks. I know what you mean, I'm discovering new places to sweat from."

The blonde was maybe a couple of inches taller than me, but our short statures were all we had in common. Her bikini barely covered anything, and she certainly had an hourglass figure to show off. Standing next to her, I looked like a board. She was exactly Jaxon's type. In fact, they had looked really cozy at dinner with the way they had been so close to each other, whispering. They had looked like a fairytale couple, all blonde and beautiful. I tried not to resent her for that; Jaxon wasn't mine.

Jaxon messed with your head. And he still was. I couldn't seem to dislodge thoughts of him no matter how hard I tried. After what I'd just learned, it should have been easy.

"Mmmm, that man is ho-ot." Nikki watched as Jaxon disappeared into the elevator. "He's ahh-mazing in bed, right? I mean I've had plenty of men in my bed, but that man knows his way around a woman's body. He plum wore me out. Oh, we'll have to dish about it with Maya later. I think he humped the stick right outta her ass."

She laughed, the sound grating on my too-raw nerves. Heat spilled across my chest, and it took all of my training not to karate-chop Barbie's head off. I forced a smile. "If I ever land a notch on that bedpost, I'll let you know."

Her smile turned vicious for a moment before her lips pulled down in a sympathetic pout. She swept my body with a pitying look. "Don't you worry, Eros is making the rounds. I'm sure he'll get to you. Eventually."

My clenched hands were sweating. I wanted to demand she deny everything she'd said, but what if it was true? I hadn't seen him with anyone else, but Jaxon was a constant flirt.

"Oh here, I think you dropped this." Nikki bent down to pick up the clothes that Jaxon had brought. Her swimsuit strained beneath the weight of her breasts and I saw way more of her than I ever wanted to see.

She held up a silky rainbow-colored swimsuit. "Oh honey, this is going to look *good* on you. Someone sure knows what suits you. Ha ha. Get it, *suit,* like swimsuit?"

"Yeah. That's a good one." I managed a small smile. "I should probably go change." I drank the rest of the water and handed her back the goblet. "Thanks again for the water."

"You're welcome. Us girls have to stick together. Good grief, you would think these boys never get out of this cave the way they look at us."

"Uh, ha. 'Good grief,' that's an oxymoron," I blurted awkwardly, not knowing what else to say.

"They *are* morons, aren't they? Especially that kid, Chris. He's so desperate, it's pathetic." Her nose scrunched up in distaste. "I don't think I've met Oxy. Which one is he?"

She can't be serious. She stared at me expectantly. Guess she is.

"An oxymoron is ... You know what, I think he's one of the servers. Uh, the short, bald one. Yeah, you probably want to stay away."

"Awww, you're so sweet!" Suddenly there was way too

much half-naked girl pressed against me. "We're gonna be best friends, I can just tell. Oh, there's Maya. I wanted to talk to her about something. See you at the race!"

She bounced off toward the scowling Asian woman in a black one-piece. How come she had gotten the conservative swimsuit and we got the skimpy ones? Of course, Nikki would probably be up for wearing our birthday suits. But I wasn't used to showing this much skin. Since my guide had abandoned me, there was no one to complain to, but I was putting in a request for something a bit more concealing.

I changed in the restrooms and tried to hide behind every tree on my way to the water. The halter top left my flat stomach bare. Only two straps held it in place; one behind my neck and the other tied at the middle of my back. At least the bottoms covered everything, but I still wanted a robe.

I picked up the pace when I heard Devon call out, "Take your places."

18

A man-made wall bisected the lagoon in front of me, rising a few inches above the surface and continuing down into the depths. Six circles were cut into the wall, the first row a couple of inches below the surface. Then other rows going down deeper and deeper. The water was so clear, I counted down to the third row of circles before it started getting dark. I could only just see the other two rows of circles beneath, the lights around these openings barely penetrating the darkness.

Molly joined me by the edge of the lagoon where I stood on the symbol of the red flying arrow that was etched into the rock. She gave me an assessing look but didn't say anything. I was sure Jaxon had filled her in on at least some of what had happened. "Your grandmother said to tell you hello. And that the water is yours to control as well."

Molly had visited my grandmother several times now. She couldn't tell me where she was or when she would be released, but she relayed messages between us.

"I can't believe it. She's encouraging me to cheat."

Molly chuckled. Ever since she had been spending time

with my grandmother, she seemed a little lighter, a little less burdened by whatever had happened to her. "Yeah, she is. 'No shame in winning however you can,' is what she said. She fights dirty. The guards are terrified of her. She's my hero."

"Any updates on when I can see her?"

It was the same question I asked every time. I didn't expect a different response, so I was surprised when Molly said, "The Kyrion have verified their story. They'll be released today."

"Really? How did the 'verification' work exactly?" Bitterness seeped into my voice. "Did Jaxon go digging around in their brains too? Or maybe you tortured it out of them? There's probably a dungeon in this place. A little torture before breakfast. Followed by watching idiots run around doing crazy competitions for your money in the evenings."

"*I* didn't do anything to them," Molly said defensively. "You know the Kyrion make the decisions around here. Not me. I do what I'm told. Generally. Anyway, they're fine. They've been staying in extra rooms on the servants' floor." She eyed me like I had been possessed. "Since when did Rainbow Bright go to the dark side?"

I breathed a sigh of relief. "Sorry. You've been great about bringing me messages from my grandmother. Thank you for that. I didn't mean to go off on you. Ever since Jaxon told me about wiping my memories, I don't feel like I can trust my own instincts. I mean, there has been so much going on. I feel like I'm losing my mind. To find out I really have lost some of it ..."

"Shit. I didn't know that part," she said, confirming they had at least talked. "Yeah, that's bad. I'd be more than grumpy."

Molly shifted uncomfortably. "Look, this is not my thing,

but Jaxon is like a brother to me. He's an idiot sometimes. But he's a good guy. One of the best I know. I, well, just wanted to say ... hang in there. Yeah, he flirts—"

I snorted thinking of what Nikki said about him sleeping with all those girls. "That's an understatement."

"But it hasn't been anything more than that for months now. Since he came back from Port Lawson, the first time." She continued to ignore me. "I think that's because of you. Just don't break his heart, ok? You're starting to grow on me too, and I really don't want to have to kill you."

She walked away, leaving me with my mouth hanging open. That couldn't be true. What about Nikki and Maya? I started to go after her, but Devon yelled at me to stay on my mark.

"Good luck," I smiled to Mikhail who stood to my left.

He just grunted and said, "Don't need it."

Ok, then. I turned to Kade on my other side, his brows were furrowed as he cast a dark look over my shoulder. "I'm sorry 'bout him, ma'am. He doesn't know how to speak to a lady."

Mikhail laughed. "What lady?"

Kade took a step toward him, but I held up my hand. "Thanks, but I can handle it. Ok?"

"If you say so, ma'am." Kade dipped his head toward me. "Let me know if you want me to take care of it, though."

"Yep." I tried not to roll my eyes. Why did no one believe I could take care of myself? It was really annoying. "Please don't ma'am me. I feel like a little old lady with a billion cats. Only one cat so far, so Dia is just fine."

"Sorry, ma—Dia." He gave me a crooked smile. "I would never mistake you for a little old lady. Cats or not."

"Are you flirting with me, Kade?"

"No, ma'am," he grinned.

I tilted my head to get a better look at my would-be rescuer. His ginger hair and beard were neatly trimmed. His baby blues held a gentle light that immediately had me relaxing. His toned chest was a lighter shade than his arms and face. His muscular thighs strained the legs of a pair of tight green board shorts. I could see why Lia call him Cowboy Cutie.

"Pardon?" He struggled not to laugh.

Oh crap, my thought-to-speech filter is broken. Again. I gave him a sheepish look.

"She nicknamed me 'Cowboy Cutie?'" He laughed. "I reckon it could be worse."

"Yep, it totally could. Lia once nicknamed a boy in our art history class 'Houdini Peni.' No, you don't want to know." I held up my hand when he opened his mouth. "Let's just say it was a date gone really wrong. The poor guy was laughed at the rest of the year for his 'disappearing penis.'"

"She certainly leaves an impression." Kade stared at the water for a moment as if reliving his own memories of Lia. *Uh oh, I hope he isn't in love with her.* I was pretty sure Bennett was never going to let her near the dating pool again. When he looked back at me, I was relieved to see he only seemed concerned. "It's a damn shame she got injured in the chariot race and can't compete. How's she doing?"

"I ..." Tears pricked my eyes. Molly had confirmed Lia was no longer on the island. Why did that make me want to cry? I knew now that she hadn't been part of the decision to wipe my memories, but she had still lied to me. "I don't know. We had a fight, and she left."

Kade gently took my hand between his and rubbed his calloused fingers along the back. "I don't know her well, but I'd be willing to bet you she'll be back. She didn't strike me as the type to give up. 'Specially not on her friends. You'll work this out."

"Thank you. I-I hope you're right."

"I'm sure y—" Kade was cut off by a shrill whistle echoing through the cavern.

Devon, the leader of the guides, stepped in front of the contestants. His dark, muscular frame loomed over us. "Today you will practice the water maze. There will be five rounds. You will swim through the tunnels starting at the top of the wall and going deeper each time. The winner will be the person who is first back to the shore for the majority of the races."

Devon's hard gaze scanned the group. "Do not go beyond the black markers on the other side of the wall. There will be a resting period before lap five. Your Kyrion will be viewing the training from the observation room below. Represent your Houses well, and you may be granted one boon from them."

Kade and I exchanged a quick "Good luck," then put on our goggles.

Devon stepped to the side. "Mark. Set. Go!"

I dived into the water and swam for my tunnel. The water was surprisingly warm, and I had a smooth rhythm going. Right before I reached the walls, I bumped into someone. I turned to see Mikhail's furious face. He bumped me and pointed to the wall. Oh. I had been heading toward his tunnel instead of my own. I tried to mime an "I'm sorry," but he darted away.

I angled toward my own tunnel and noticed everyone else had already made it through. *This is only the first round. Don't worry about it.* If I tired myself out trying to catch up now, I wouldn't have anything left for the other rounds. The rock surrounded me for a brief moment as I passed through the tunnel, thankful that I wasn't claustrophobic. I was the last to return to the shore.

I tried again to apologize to Mikhail, but he sneered and told me to keep out of his way.

The next tunnel was slightly longer and a couple of feet below the first row of tunnels. I made it through quickly and won that round. On the third round, we all spent a few more minutes getting our breath back when we surfaced on the other side of the wall. My smaller form was coming in handy with being able to maneuver through the tunnels quickly, and I won another round.

My blood pumped through my veins furiously, sounding like waves in my ears as I tried to calm myself for round four. Luckily, they gave us a few minutes to catch our breath. Then we were off again, going even deeper. My lungs burned for air. Suddenly the lights that outlined the tunnels took on a yellow-green hue. Flashes of light burst in my periphery like I was the centerpiece of a photo shoot. My vision wavered, and the tunnels tripled, then were back to normal before doubling. I aimed toward the nearest tunnel and closed my eyes.

I bumped into something and was roughly shoved into the wall. My knee scraped against the stone. My hands scrambled to find the opening for the tunnel, but only found solid wall. *Where is the dang opening?* I widened my search and finally found what I was looking for. I dove through the tunnel, this one almost as long as my body length, and fought toward the surface. I broke the surface with a gasp as I greedily sucked down air. I could hear Devon calling out the names of those who had made it back to shore, but I was solely focused on trying to make my lungs feel like they weren't collapsing. Somehow, I made it back to shore and lay there on the hard rock panting.

A scuffle sounded close by. Mikhail's angry voice was shouting about me trying to drown him. Kade was threatening to teach him not to lay his hands on women. Then Devon's deep voice joined in, breaking it up. Gentle hands rolled me over.

"Dia! Dia, are you ok?" Molly's concerned voice echoed through my pounding head causing me to wince and try to roll away. "Hey, stop rolling around. We don't have long. You need to get it together. One more round, that's all you need. Dia? Dia, are you hearing me?"

"Kitties don't like water."

"Stop making jokes and get up. You need to be ready for this next round." Molly grabbed my elbow and pulled me to my feet. A blue halo surrounded her. I poked a finger at it but hit empty air. "Damnit, are you drunk? I'm going to roast Jaxon's balls like chestnuts if he liquored you up."

"No touching his balls!" I said with a giggle. "Those're mine to fud ... fond ... You know what I mean."

"Right. Ok then, up you go."

"Molly, I don't feel so good."

She sighed. "This is what happens when you let a descendant of a god of passion into your panties. I'm never falling in love."

"Not in my panties. Been in everyone else's." I swayed into her, and she grunted. "Never say never. Captain Jack could clear the cobwebs from your girl parts. I've seen him in an *itty-bitty* towel. If you don't want him, I'm int ... inrest ... I'll take him."

"Not happening!" She cinched her arm around me, and we hobbled forward. "Stop giggling. It's not because I want him. Jaxon would go all big-brother trying to protect my non-existent virtue. He'd shoot Jack with an arrow. And not the fall-in-love kind. As annoying as Jack is, I don't want to see him hurt."

"Liar, liar, crotch on fire!"

"Shut up before someone thinks I have an STD."

"Stick-up-your-butt disorder?"

"That would be SUYBD," she grumbled under her breath. "Did you inhale too much salt water or something? Just stop talking."

"Oh look, there's Jaxon. Isn't he so pretty?"

"Yeah, dreamy." She shifted her grip, pulling me more upright. "Don't look now, but your man is heading this way. I would say run, but you would fall on your face."

I waved at Jaxon as he approached with a scowl on his face. I stumbled forward and brushed my hand through his hair. There was some reason why I was supposed to be mad at him, but I couldn't remember. A pink-and-white tiger lily grew from the palm of my hand. Jaxon grabbed my hand pulling it down between us, "What're you doing? The other contestants will see you."

"A pretty flower for a pretty man." I laughed. Then pushed his hair back behind one ear and tucked the flower in his hair. "I don't like you, but I do. The nice you, not the playboy you. He probably has more miles on him than my Prius."

Molly laughed.

Jaxon groaned. "You're being a very bad, Tigerlily. But maybe I should take advantage while you're not hating me. Will you meet me in my rooms tonight for our first date?"

"Nope, I'm a good girl." I launched myself into his arms. He was so surprised he barely caught me. "You're the bad boy. But I can be bad too. Wanna see?"

"I'm going to take this as a 'yes' to the date."

Jaxon gulped as my fingers trailed down his red silk shirt

to the snap of his jeans. His breath hissed in, followed by a moan. His eyes rounded as I traced his zipper, and he gave Molly a wide-eyed look.

"Don't ask me. She came out of the water this way."

Jaxon gripped both my hands in his, then took a step back. "I think I—ah, you—need a cold shower ... I mean, water. You need to drink some cold water and rest." He gulped again when I pressed myself against him. "The race. Need to focus on the race."

"Not a race." I leaned up on my tiptoes to lick his collarbone. "When I get you naked I want it to be slow and last all night. I'll make you want me."

He made a choking sound, then suddenly he was gone. Wind whipped around us, tugging strands of hair from my braid and causing my nipples to harden even further. It sounded like his voice on the wind saying, "I already do."

Molly squirted cold water all over me causing me to squeal. She smiled mischievously, then handed me the bottle. "Cool down before one of you spontaneously combusts."

We lined up at the water's edge once more. My head and stomach felt like I'd drunk my paycheck in half-priced margaritas. Molly had forced me to drink a bunch of water and lay down for a few minutes. I couldn't say I was back to normal, but I could walk a straight line. That would have to be good enough for now because I was determined to win this one. Only one more race and I was in the lead.

Jaxon had come back but kept his distance. Mostly he grumbled that he was retracting his earlier statement about complicated not being a bad thing. He paced around the side of the lagoon, refusing to go back down to the observation area. I ignored him and worked through a couple of yoga poses to center myself.

When the whistle sounded this time, I dove deep, my focus on reaching the tunnel first to get ahead. The water pressure grew: it felt like I was swimming through heavy cream. My lungs strained desperately, wanting me to take a breath. The faint light of the tunnel was my only guide this far down. I was a foot away from the tunnel when something hit me from the side. Air burst from my lungs like the cork from a bottle, and it took every ounce of will I had not to gasp in liquid death.

Shark! I sank toward the rocky bottom of the lagoon hoping to find a place to hide.

A dark shape zoomed past me, and I felt something grab my butt. Sharks don't try to cop a feel. *Mikhail.* It had to be him. *Was he trying to kill me or take me out of the race?* It didn't matter because my lungs were nearly out of air and my shoulder—which had taken the brunt of the hit—was throbbing painfully.

This is how a life ends. Not in an explosion of colors like the setting of the sun but lost to the murky depths where light barely penetrates.

No! I had fought my whole life not to be like my mother used to be. I wasn't giving up now. *I will not die.*

Determination filled me, and some instinct took over. I pressed my lips to the rock floor, and, using the last of my breath, I blew until there was nothing left. The ground shifted beneath me and expanded like a balloon forming a protective cocoon around me. The water rushed out like a geyser through the small hole above me before it closed completely. I was in a rock bubble only a little larger than my crouched form. I gulped in air thirstily, my head pounding and my stomach churning. Everything I had ever eaten seemed to suddenly make a reappearance as I heaved onto the rock beneath me. Thankfully, the noxious piles were swallowed by the rock leaving me with only fresh air.

I sat back on my knees and pulled my swimming goggles off to rub my eyes. Maybe if I kept my eyes shut the darkness wouldn't bother me. My breath started to come more rapidly as memories filled my mind. The hot summer days of my childhood locked in the small dark apartment, the sound of my mother's crying my only company.

Stop it! You aren't there. You aren't a helpless child anymore. Think. You can get yourself out of this.

My focus turned inward, sinking down to the core of myself. A vibrant green ball of light filled my mind. Then a second bluish-white ball. Then a tiny red ball. They dipped and weaved around each other. The green ball drew my attention and I reached out. A drop of green melted from the ball like wax and coated my fingertip. The smell of dirt and rain washed through me. My senses came alive with the sound and feel of nature all around. I saw through the eyes of a fish as it swam over my rock cocoon. I felt the wind as it rustled the leaves of a tree somewhere on the surface.

A newfound confidence filled me. I touched my finger to the rock in front of me and a glowing green mushroom unfurled. Then another and another.

The fear that had always lingered in the back of my mind that I would one day sink into the darkness of depression and never return, disappeared. I laughed, feeling like a giant weight had been lifted from me. The sound echoed around the small space and the mushrooms swayed as if sharing in my joy.

I knew exactly what to do now. I pressed my hand to the rock and it peeled back like a banana. I stood, and the water shifted out of my way. I walked across the lagoon floor, my air pocket secure around me. Then I closed my rock cocoon back up, securing a safe spot for the mushrooms to grow. I placed my goggles back on and let the water lift me up. The race was probably over, but I would finish what I started.

I let the water slowly fill in around me and swam for one of the tunnels.

Then I was through and swimming for the surface on the other side of the wall. I came up gasping and was surprised to find the rest of the contestants still in the water by the black markers marking off the training area. The tension in the air was thick. Kade called out to me, but a loud whistle cut off whatever he said. I realized they must have paused the race while I was trapped in my rock cocoon. I hurriedly took a deep breath and back down I went.

I was halfway there when my vision went blurry again and pain lanced through my temples. Had I hit my head when I was making my rock cocoon?

I didn't think so, but there was something wrong. I made it back to the tunnel and pushed inside. The lights of the tunnel surrounded me, their white glow changing to that sickly yellow-green color. This tunnel was twice as long as any of the others, and it felt like forever before I exited out the other end. My foot grazed the wall by accident, but I took the opportunity to push off it. I pushed hard toward the surface, my shoulder protesting every stroke. The ache turned to burning, but I ignored it. Flashes of light sailed past me. The blue water took on a muddy brown color. My lungs screamed for one breath—just one. A cramp seized my belly, and bile filled my mouth. I chocked it back down, the foul taste making me want to gag.

Heaviness settled in my limbs, my heart beating like an out-of-control locomotive as I struggled to keep moving. I strained my blurry vision to make out the shoreline of the lagoon only feet away. Almost there. I broke the surface, but everything was lost to swirling lights. Shouts sounded, and I focused on moving toward them. My hand scraped against rock and that was the last thing I knew as white light closed around me.

20

My skin prickled painfully in the cold. All around me gray fog swirled. Keening wails echoed through the damp air. My stomach clenched at the sounds that were so similar to those of my childhood.

"Hello," I called. "Is anyone there?"

The wails changed to heart-wrenching sobs. Maybe this time would be different. Maybe this time I could help my mother out of that dark place that claimed her. "It's ok. I'm here."

"You left me," a small voice whispered. That wasn't my mother's hoarse voice telling me to go back to bed. I looked around. The dingy hallway of the apartment where I had grown up was nowhere in sight. "Where am I?"

"Thanatos," the small tear-choked voice answered.

"That sounds like a toe fungus," I mumbled. "What's a 'thanatos?'"

"This place. The shadowlands of the dead." A hiccuping sob sounded. "You chose the Goddess, not me."

"Who are you?"

"Meara," she sniffled.

"You tried to turn me into a popsicle! What was I supposed to do?"

"I didn't mean to!" she cried. "I was trying to protect you. He tried to follow you through the portal, but I wouldn't let him. Now it's too late. He knows you're alive."

"Who knows I'm alive?"

The ghost child I had seen in the Emerald Rain Forest materialized through the gray swirling clouds. She sat with her knees clutched to her chest, big sad eyes glistening with tears. Though she was made up of grays like the landscape, she seemed more solid here. "He will twist the truth around until you're too confused to know what it is. He will ask you to do things, and you'll want to do them to make him proud. He's so nice when you've made him proud."

"Are you saying there's a bad man coming for me?"

She nodded. "He can visit here too. He's been searching here for a very long time, but I'm good at hiding. You have to learn to hide too."

"Please, Meara, I don't understand any of this. Can you explain it to me?"

The silence stretched on for several moments before the child said petulantly, "I could show you, but you locked me out. You locked us all out."

"What do you mean?"

"You put up the wall, and I can't get to your thoughts anymore." She nodded her head toward the swirling mists. "This is the in-between place where people go after they die to wait for judgment. The others aren't like me. Most don't know they are dead yet. They want to keep living and you offer them a way. Your mind has always been wide open. You could listen to the real world and this one at the same time. I keep them from getting into you, but I can't stop their voices."

"The constant noise in my head. The random thoughts. Are you saying I've been listing to the ghost hotline?"

"Yes, you have always been able to hear the shades. Most pass on and never notice you. Others ... they want their life back. They think you can give it to them. I protected you." There was such a pained look of betrayal on her little face. "You shut the door. No one can get through. Not even me."

"I don't want to be possessed!" I shouted. Moans sounded nearby, and I lowered my voice. "Not by ghosts or a goddess. I just want to be me. Is that so hard to understand?"

"No." She clutched her braid staring at the ground. "I've been with you since you were a baby. Tucked away in your head. Living through you as much as I could. I know what it's like to want to be yourself."

I closed my eyes imagining being a ghost inside another person with limited ability to interact with the outside world and your host completely unaware of you. It sounded like hell.

"I can't image what you've gone through. But if you help me find answers and get out of this place"—Careful, Dia, there was no going back from this decision—"I'll do what I can to help you too."

"Do ... Do you mean it?" Meara stared at me with cautious hope.

"I pinky promise. You know how serious I take those. Partners?"

She nodded and floated forward to wrap her cold little finger around my own. "I pinky promise to help you too. Partners."

Her smile bloomed and she hugged me. "Yay! We're going to have so much fun. I can show you how to walk Thanatos and view through other ghosts. Not that you need much help since you've already done that. But there are so many of us. We're gonna be bestist friends like when you were little."

"My invisible friend, that was you?" Meara nodded. "Mom thought I was talking to the Great Mother. She would be so disappointed."

Meara's shoulders slumped and her head dropped.

"I didn't mean she would be disappointed that you were my friend," I hastily reassured her.

She gave me a small smile then held out her hand. "We're still connected, but you have to remove the block so I can show you."

"What about the other ghosts?"

"Don't worry, they won't get to you," she said confidently.

Hesitantly, I slipped my hand into her much smaller one. "Uh, what are you going to show me?"

She giggled. "Once upon a time ... That's where all stories start."

"Right." A bluish-white light flared between our joined hands and the shadows swirled around us. My head felt like it was being sucked through my feet as we were swept away. Then we were crashing through a thick forest, a white glow around a small fist, the only thing I could see. "What's happening?"

"We're reliving my memories," Meara said calmly as she ran frantically through a dark forest. "Africa is the territory of Gaia—of the House of Seasons. Their home base is here, deep in the Congo. And so is the village where I grew up, Chaméni Elpída."

The name hit me like a ton of bricks. We were going back to the village that had been attacked. I shivered, and it wasn't from the cold.

Tree limbs smacked into Meara's face and tore at her clothes as she ran. Then, suddenly, she hurtled away from the forest into the gray mists of Thanatos. My head spun at the unexpected change. Then she was back in the forest again. "Don't be scared," Meara soothed, "we're not really here now."

"It seems pretty real to me."

She giggled. "You'll get used to it. Then you'll be able to connect with ghosts even when you aren't asleep."

She popped in and out of Thanatos, the scenery changing rapidly. "I learned to walk the shadowlands whenever I chose that night. Fear taught me what my father tried to force. I used Thanatos to travel over two thousand miles to get back to my family. To warn them."

"What?"

"Thanatos isn't like Earth. Time is slower. You can move over long distances with a thought, but it takes a lot of power."

Meara finally stopped at the edge of the forest, gasping for air. Chaméni Elpída sat in the clearing in the distance. Only the village looked very different. The huts were well maintained. A large garden spread out across a field on one side. Livestock filled fenced areas. A drum beat as shadows danced around a large fire. Laughter rang out as children chased each other. "This is what my tribe once was. They only wanted a simple life. Working and living close to the Goddess. That's why they left the House of Seasons. Our village was declared outcast, no longer under the protection of the Kyrion, but we were free to live as we chose. I didn't understand that then. There was so much I didn't understand."

Meara ducked low to the ground and moved closer to the village. "It's time for the story," she said softly. "Once upon a time there was a beautiful chieftain's daughter who was very powerful. She lived in this village deep in the Congo where no outsiders were allowed. But the girl wanted to see more of the world. She disobeyed her father and went out to explore the forests.

"One day she met a man who was also very powerful. They met many times as they explored their powers together and love grew between them. They promised themselves to each other knowing their families would not approve. Then the day came when the chieftain demanded his daughter take a husband. The girl refused and admitted she was with child. The chieftain was very angry and said his daughter would live apart from the tribe as a lowly gatherer. She didn't mind so much because she could meet with her love without the watchful eyes of the warriors."

Here, Meara tripped and fell. She sobbed harder but got back up. "When I was born the midwife told the chieftain of the mark on my back. Mother was welcomed back into the tribe. Her status was raised to protector of the village and Father was allowed to visit. He always brought gifts and new things for me to learn. We were happy."

"Then Father visited less. When he did come, he wanted only for me to practice my powers. He was angry when I couldn't do it right. My eleventh year he did not come for my birth celebration. I blamed Mother." Regret filled Meara's voice. "I told her she drove Father away. I screamed at her that I hated her."

The sound of her sobs was joined by her name being called and she ran faster. "Father came to visit weeks later, and I begged him to take me with him. We left in the middle of the night without a word to Mother."

Her voice rang with a bitterness way beyond her years. "He took me to his family home, Phàsia Castle in Mauritania," she said. "I wish I had never gone with him. It's a cold, evil place."

Meara's scrawny legs pumped furiously as she raced toward a hut separated from the others. The thatched roof had haphazard sections of straw piled upon it as if someone had thrown it there for repair but never gotten around to completing the task. Gaps could be seen through the branches that made up the walls.

She cautiously pushed aside the animal-skin door. A woman lay curled on a reed mat in the dim light of the hut. Meara dropped to her knees beside the woman and brushed the dark hair from her cheek. Language poured from her lips that I didn't know but understood nonetheless.

"Mother, I am sorry," Meara sobbed. "Please forgive me."

The woman rolled onto her back, and shock hit me like stepping off the edge of a cliff. I was in free-fall and terrified of what would be waiting for me at the bottom. How could she be here? The woman on the mat was a much younger version, but the face was the same. It was a face I had looked at every day growing up. One less lined with age and bitter disappointments, but there was a darkness in her eyes that I knew all too well. It was small, not the all-consuming darkness she had fought when I was a child. But there was no mistaking this was my mother.

"Meara." *She blinked up at the girl with a sleep-confused expression. Suddenly, she sat up gripping her in a crushing hug.* "My daughter. My daughter. You have returned."

Daughter? But I was her only daughter. Right?

"I love you, Mother. I'm sorry for leaving."

"Hush, child, there is nothing to apologize for. I have missed you sorely." *Mother kissed her head, and the girl snuggled into her.* "It is me who is sorry, daughter. I should not have denied you use of your power or tried to force you to be someone you are not. You have the fierce heart of your father. I should have known I could not hold you back."

"No, Mother, you were right. The powers draw the bad people. We must leave." *Meara sprang to her feet and tugged at my mother's hands.* "Father is coming. He'll bring the bad people."

"Your father is coming?" *Mother began to fiddle with her hair.*

"Mother, we must go," *Meara urged.* "Father is part of the bad people. He brings them here now to destroy the village."

"Nonsense. What has he been teaching you? Your father wants a different future for us, but he would never hurt our people."

"Mother, please, you must believe me. They call themselves the House of Spirits. I heard him tell the commander-at-arms that they would attack the village. He wants to kill everyone. He called us 'useless Chaonian-halflings.'"

The color bled from Mother's face. "The House of Spirits? You are sure?"

"Yes, he—" A baby cried out nearby.

Mother quickly stood and rushed to a pile of cloth in the corner. She scooped up the baby and rocked it in her arms. "Come meet your sister."

"M-My sister?"

No, it couldn't be! Dread and anxiety swirled in my stomach. The overwhelming combination that had filled too many of my days as a child. If I had been in my own body I would probably be throwing up.

"I was with child when your father left. This is Dalia."

My mother called me "flower." Is this why? Not because I talked to the flowers so much when I was little, but because my real name was that of a flower.

Meara cautiously approached the squirming bundle. There nestled in the cloths was a tiny baby. Her eyes were a vivid blue with a thatch of blondish-brown hair. "How old is she?"

"Five months. We feared for her health because she is so small, but Dalia is a fighter."

Meara reached out to the waving arms, and tiny fingers gripped hers. The crying stopped. A green light flared around the twined fingers, and a perfect pink flower petal floated to the ground. "She ... She is like me."

My thoughts were a mess. But I knew one thing for sure. That baby was me.

"Her markings are different," Mother said, "but, yes, she is like you."

"He can't find her, Mother!" Meara's eyes were big and scared as she stared at the baby. "He'll try to turn her. We have to—"

An eerie wail sounded. Meara gripped Mother's arm tightly. "They are here."

"I love you, daughter." Mother pulled Meara into a hug. "Here

take your sister and hide in the forest. The Great Mother will protect you."

"My mark is of spirit, like Father. How will the Great Mother hear me?"

"The Great Mother answers those with a pure heart. You need only call her, Meara."

"What about you? Come with us."

"I am the protector. I must see to the others. It is the burden of the powerful, as you already know." Mother brushed a kiss across the girl's head and then the baby's. *"Go now. Be safe my daughters."*

Meara edged out of the hut and sprinted for the woods. A plea was on repeat in her head for the Great Mother to keep them safe. She stumbled in the dark woods, the baby getting heavier by the minute. Then she leaned against a large tree to rest. The baby's hand brushed the tree, and green sparks flew. A green I recognized as my powers as the sparks dipped and weaved through the air, then sped off in different directions, only to return moments later to circle the girls.

That had been a whole lot of lights. I'd managed to create maybe a dozen glowing mushrooms. Had I been even more powerful as a baby?

Meara watched as the sparks came together to form a swarming mass like lightning bugs. They tugged at her braids and clothes. "You want me to follow you?" she asked. The lights vibrated happily in the air, a few darting off to the left and racing back. "Ok. Ok. I am coming."

Meara walked for several minutes following the little green lights until she came to a thicket. The brush shifted from her path to reveal an opening in the underbrush barely big enough to lay down in. She settled down with the baby cradled against her as the bushes weaved themselves into a protective bubble around them. She must have fallen asleep because the next thing she knew there was a huge hand wrapped around her neck dragging her up into the air.

A massive man with fire leaping from his eyes held her in the air, and no matter how hard she struggled she couldn't get free. "Paden thinks you are something special. But you are worthless like all Chaonian halflings. Better to rid our House of your disgrace."

It was so quick there was no time to react. One moment the moon was glinting off the blade and next it was buried in Meara's chest. She screamed in agony. The giant tossed her to the ground like trash and reached for the baby. "Another bastard child of Paden's? I will rid the world of you both."

Meara flung herself over the baby and pressed her lips to the baby's shoulder. I could hear in her thoughts that she had no clue why she was doing this, but only wanted to save her sister. As Meara's life drained away a symbol formed on the baby's shoulder. A white symbol of a three-headed dog. It glowed a bluish-white color and everywhere the light touched became coated in frost. I could feel Meara's life slip away and into the baby's body.

The looming giant hesitated a moment then shook the frost away and pulled a second knife from his fatigue pants. He plunged the blade toward the baby. Before it made contact a tree picked him up and threw him into the night. Mother appeared. Her long hair was streaked with soot. Her clothes were ripped, and a patch of blood coated her side. She dropped to her knees and pulled Meara's lifeless body into her lap. Her keening cry filled the night and leaves rained down as the forest wept alongside her. She begged over and over again for Meara to come back to her.

That was the cry that woke me from my sleep nearly every night as a child. I understood now the nightmares that haunted my mother. She refused to talk about my father, so I had always assumed he was the reason she was so sad. Regret filled me.

Having lived through her past now with Meara, I realized how very strong my mother truly was.

"That was how we were joined," Meara said as we returned to Thanatos. "You are marked with spirit and with earth. I do not know what Gaia plans for you, but I will be here for you sister as I always have been."

21

"Her blood tested positive for digitalis poisoning." The tired-sounding voice filtered through to my comfy land of dreams. "You're lucky I recognized the symptoms so quickly. The amount of time it had been in her system, combined with the activity from the swimming races, had moved the poison through her body quickly. There doesn't appear to be any permanent damage, but only time will tell. What she needs now is rest."

"Thank you, doctor." Jaxon said. "I'll make sure she gets the rest she needs. She'll be a guest here on my floor until she has recovered. I've already informed her servants."

Their voices trailed off as they left the room.

I drifted in that in-between sleep place until what they were talking about registered. *I was poisoned? And Jaxon was making decisions for me!*

I sat up in bed and my head felt like it exploded. I got a brief impression of a small bedroom with bare walls and basic furniture before my vision went blurry. A strong arm wrapped around my back and eased me down onto the bed.

Jaxon's spiced wine smell teased my senses and I wanted to curl up in his arms. "Careful, Dia. You've been out for a while."

Tears slipped from the corners of my eyes as the pain continued to pound in my head.

"Here, the doctor left you some pills for the headache."

I refused to let him feed me the pills like I was a helpless child, and he reluctantly gave in.

I closed my eyes as if I could pretend I'd never overheard the conversation but opened them a moment later. I wouldn't hide from the truth. Jaxon had been right about me being like him—the truth no matter how bad, was better than living with a lie. "Is it true? Did someone poison me?"

He waited until my gaze met his. "Yes, it's true. The guides are going over the training area for any clues. Did anything strange happen this morning? Did you eat or drink anything different?"

It was a struggle to remember everything at first, but eventually the morning came back to me. I'd had breakfast in my rooms as usual. Then gone to the training area. I'd snuck into the meadow to pull a few snacks from the stump. Then the race. The only other thing had been the water Nikki had brought me, but that was ridiculous. She was more likely to sleep with your boyfriend than try to kill someone.

"No, I can't think of anything."

Jaxon quizzed me about my day until my belly growled like it was going to eat him. He brought me a tray of food, and I felt a little better after eating. We argued again when I wanted to go to the bathroom by myself. We bargained: I would stay here in his guest room if he stopped trying to baby me.

I took advantage of my few minutes alone in the bathroom to take a quick shower, but underestimated how much it would sap my energy. I was sitting on the closed toilet lid trying to work up the strength to dry off when Jaxon walked in. He ignored my yelling at him while I tried to cover the important parts of my nakedness and dried me off in a detached kind of way—as though I was his kid sister. It made me feel like I was completely undesirable. I mean, the man was working his way through the female population of the island and didn't even try to look at me when I was naked.

I was hurt and embarrassed. I snarled at him as he carried me back to bed that I could take care of myself and I didn't want him here. He'd leaned down and captured my lips in a tender kiss. That confused me. I was telling him that this wasn't working as I slipped back to sleep.

"*Dia, wake up.*" The voice floated through my head and I grunted.

"Argh, not yet," I mumbled.

A hand rested on my face. "Sto-op!"

The hand pulled off my face, and I rolled over, snuggling into my pillow. Then a stinging smack landed on my butt. "Oomph."

I twisted around to find my own hand resting on my butt. Giggles filled my head.

I rolled over and draped my arms across my face. The oversized T-shirt that must have come from Jaxon slid up to the tops of my thighs. "Ha ha. Very funny making me smack my own butt."

"I thought so." Meara giggled again. "You've been sleeping for hours and I'm bored."

"This ghost in my head thing is going to take some getting used to," I groaned, as I carefully got out of bed. "Can you haunt the kitchen and scare me up some food?"

Meara appeared in her ghostly form in front of me and blew a raspberry. "No, but Jaxon had your servants set up a whole snack bar over on that table. And put your clothes in the closet."

I shuffled across the floor, thankful that my head was feeling better. I stopped in front of the table giving a girly little squeal as I spotted some of my favorites. The man had scored major forgiveness points for this. It was like my own concession stand of yummy goodness. There were baskets of Skittles, Nerds, and Strawberry Shortcake Rolls. On the other side were veggies and fruits arranged like flowers.

"Hurry up. I want to try something."

"Stop rushing me." I grabbed two plates and started piling them up. "Is this what it's like having a sister?"

"I don't know." Meara hesitated before saying, "I guess we'll learn together."

"Guess so," I mumbled around my snack cake.

She laughed. "You look silly. Get a napkin."

"*Bossy.*" I switched to talking to her in my mind. Now I could eat and talk with my mouth full.

"I am twelve years older than you, you know," Meara stated imperiously.

I worked my way around the table tasting a little of everything, until my stomach called uncle. I swayed on my feet as I made my way back to the bed, feeling full and ready for another nap. The next thing I knew, my feet were carrying me to the wall of windows. I blinked sleepily in the afternoon sun, looking out on the sheer drop down to the ocean.

"How are you doing that?" I asked Meara, realizing that, like the butt smacking, I hadn't been the one driving me.

"I can control your body sometimes." She stated like it

was no big deal. "It's easiest when you're distracted or really tired."

"Yeah, let's not do that again."

"I was only having a little fun, but I won't do it again," she promised.

"Great. Now what did you have in mind to keep us from going stir-crazy?"

We spent the afternoon trying out exercises with my spirit powers. It wasn't as easy as the earth power. The green ball of earth power was like putty, wanting to be shaped and molded. The blue-white ball of light at my center kept slipping through my grip. It was like smoke, constantly shifting. I couldn't dig my hands into it like soil, I had to finesse it with my mind. By the time I declared myself too tired to continue, I'd gotten the hang of blocking Meara from my thoughts. I'd also been able to see through her eyes when she took her ghostly form and our mental communication had gotten stronger.

I had been a little surprised that Jaxon hadn't visited, but one of our experiments had been for Meara to track him down while I was seeing through her eyes. He'd been checking in with the guides on the investigation into my poisoning. The lawyer side had been out in full force as he interrogated them. It had been a bit of a turn-on to see him like that. Then I realized my reaction to him while inside Meara's head was really inappropriate. She had teased me about it all the way back to the room.

Most people would think having a child ghost permanently attached to you would be creepy. I wouldn't deny that it was taking some getting used to, but I'd been raised to embrace the spirit of Mother Nature. What was one more? The only part that really scared me was when she was able to take me over completely, but she'd promised not to do it again. I knew she meant it, but I wanted to be strong enough to keep it from ever happening again. I wanted to be strong enough to protect her too. Now that I had a better understanding of the cage she had been living in for twenty-seven years, I was determined to free my sister from her prison—me.

I took a short nap after that, and got up again, feeling stronger. I marched out of the bedroom expecting to have a fight on my hands, but Jaxon still wasn't back. I decided to go exploring.

His floor was a weird split. On the side with the bedroom where I'd slept, it looked like a fancy penthouse suite with sleek clean lines. The other side looked like the mountain had been left in its natural state. Pine trees dotted a meadow and the outcroppings of rock along the wall. A waterfall fell from a rocky ledge two stories above into a pool surrounded by a sandy beach. The outside wall of the floor was completely open to the outdoors.

I walked out onto the ledge of this outcrop, high on Mount Titan. Night was slowly creeping across the valley below. I could still see the ridge in the distance that always seemed to call to me, and my earth power seemed to dance inside me for a second. My toes wiggled at the edge of the sheer drop. It was exhilarating standing here at a precipice. One step in either direction could alter my fate. My powers swelled inside me as if encouraging me to take a leap of faith. Would I soar, or would I fall?

A breeze wrapped around me and pulled me from the ledge. My feet dangled several inches off the ground as I was spun around. Jaxon stood in the opening of his rooms, his expression fierce as he stared at me. He made a "come here" gesture and the wind carried me to him. This was his power.

I had wondered. The little caresses of wind whenever his eyes were on me made sense now.

"What were you doing so close to the edge?" His velvet voice commanded an answer.

I liked the lawyer in him when it was directed at others, but not so much when it was directed at me. "Did you think I was going to jump? I'm crazy, not suicidal."

"No, I was thinking someone already tried to kill you, and you're giving them another damn fine opportunity."

Oh, well, when he put it that way. "I hadn't thought of that."

Those plump lips thinned in displeasure. He held out his hand and the breeze set me down on the ground in front of him. "You have to be more careful. We don't know who was behind the poison, and don't think I've forgotten about the near-electrocution in the rain forest."

"Right, that too. I'll be careful. But I can—"

"—take care of yourself. Yes, I've heard." Jaxon turned and walked away. "I'll leave you to it."

I followed him, wondering why he was acting so strange. I shouldn't care. But there was a ton of things I shouldn't do. Like ogle his butt. I'd had plenty of time to think about my life today and the fresh perspective of near-death. Life was meant for living, and I had been so close to locking myself away because I was afraid of getting hurt again. My heart may have been bruised, but it was still beating. I was going to live to the fullest as I had always promised myself.

Jaxon entered the pine-tree meadow on the other side of his floor, his quick stride never slowing. I struggled to keep up, my body feeling the strain from nearly a whole day in bed. He came to a stop a few feet from a pine tree and held his hand back toward me, indicating I should stop. The tree was bigger than most of the others with a thick trunk and long-reaching limbs. We stood silently watching the tree. Birdsong filled the air after a few minutes and movement in the branches near the top caught my eye. A small yellow bird hopped along the branches chirping, then poking its bill into a pinecone. It hopped further along the branch to the very end to deliver the pine seed to a nest. Three grayish-yellow baby birds chirped, their mouths open wide to receive the food. A second bird came and repeated the process.

It's a whole family. Aww, they're so cute!

Minutes passed as the birds finished their meal. Then the babies hopped about their nest flapping their wings. The parents stayed nearby, their heads constantly turning to search their surroundings for danger. I dared not even breathe as they finally declared it safe, and the babies climbed out of their nest. They clung tightly to the branch and then let go. My heart was in my throat as they fell. One caught on and flew away. Then another. But the smallest one was still falling. It flapped one wing then the other but couldn't seem to find its coordination. A cry of denial was lodged in my throat as it plummeted toward the ground.

A foot from the ground a burst of wind wrapped around the bird and forced its little wings open. The wind helped the bird to find its rhythm until the little guy caught on and flew off with its family.

I stared in awe at the back of the man in front of me. That was the sweetest thing I'd ever seen anyone do. My heart melted.

"I haven't stopped thinking about what you said. About who I really am." Jaxon turned to me, his face still carefully blank. "The thing is, I've been searching for so long for who I *was*, for everything I lost as a child, that I'd never tried to understand who I *am*. My very first memory is of Bennett taking me by the hand and telling me it would be ok. He and his mother are the only real family I've ever known. My sister was …"

I swallowed thickly, imagining what he must have gone through. "I'm guessing Natalie wasn't a very nice person even before she went off the deep end."

"No, she wasn't. Especially to me. Those first years living with Bennett's family, I would cry and try to hide every time she came near. Of course, I was a traumatized three-year-old. But Nat made it worse."

"Bennett would find me in whatever hiding spot I'd crawled into and spend hours coaxing me out. He would dry my tears and give me ice cream." A small sad smile lifted the corner of his lips for a brief second. "He might have left me there if he knew that I would follow him around like a puppy most of his life with a huge case of hero worship."

"I don't really know him, but he seems the overly protective type. Like someone else I know," I said pointedly.

"I learned from the best." He combed his fingers through his hair, a rueful look in his eyes. "You're right, he wouldn't have left me. He's too damn responsible for that."

He twirled his fingers to form a mini-cyclone and tossed it from hand to hand. "My whole life I've taken the easy road. Usually, that was following wherever Bennett led. I've been more of a figurehead for the House of Arrows, never really a leader." The cyclone disappeared, and Jaxon stared over my head like he was ashamed. A lost look in his eyes that scared me. I hated that look and the self-disgust in his voice. I hated the distance between us.

Then change it, Dia. You know you want to.

"Even becoming a lawyer was partly to help Bennett out. Our people needed someone to smooth things over in the human world. I was good at research and tests came easy to me, so why not. I graduated high school at seventeen, completed my undergrad bachelor's degree in Criminal Justice, followed by three years at Harvard Law School." Anger vibrated in his voice when he mumbled, "Nothing but the best, of course, for the stepson of Dr. Jude Young."

He must have noticed my concern and his anger disappeared as if it had never been.

"Don't do that," I blurted out.

His brows furrowed in confusion. "Don't do what?"

"Hide your emotions," I said. "You were angry. Then you pasted on the happy 'nothing-could-possibly-be-wrong-with-me' face."

"Because there's nothing to tell. I'd been the Kyrion of my House since I was three, even though Dr. Young took care of the official stuff as my guardian. The Kyrion are trained from birth for their roles and are generally expected to take their thrones at the age of sixteen." He shrugged. "Bennett's dad was more of an asshole about duties than most, but it's not a big deal."

I concentrated on the grass below his feet. It grew taller and twined up his legs. Pink wildflowers bloomed as the grass reached his waist. He laughed and cussed as the grass tickled along his bare arms. A pink flower tickled him under the chin. The hopelessness that had been sinking his shoulders lower and lower was replaced by wild laughter.

When his laughter died down, I walked up to him and brushed the hair from his face. "You are more than you give yourself credit for. Molly worships the ground you walk on, and she's nobody's fool. Bennett trusts you to handle all of the lawyer-y stuff, right? I didn't see him standing over your shoulder telling you what to do when you were questioning the guides earlier." I opened my heart and let everything I felt show on my face. "I hated what you did to me, but I don't hate you. I'm scared to death by what you make me feel, and I don't know if you feel the same. How could I when you're always hiding?"

I placed a kiss on his cheek and walked away.

"Dia, get back here and get me out of this. Dia!"

22

I walked through the pine meadow toward the rocky cliff. Jaxon continued to shout at me, but I ignored him. He may not have figured out who he was, but he had a chance to decide who he wanted to be now. I was scared that he would choose to be the playboy and not the man I loved. I had finally admitted it—to myself and him. It was his turn now.

I entered one of the openings in the rock and found an archery range. The room was long and cylindrical. Lights lined the rough walls and ceiling. White bags with red targets in various sizes lined the back wall. Down each side of the wall hung bows of all sorts. Beneath them, hung rows of quivers, filled with arrows. A large black safe sat in the corner opposite the doorway.

The room crackled with energy and the air toward the end of the range seemed to waver. Jaxon appeared a second later. His faced flushed. A couple of buttons ripped off his red shirt. Pink petals in his wild hair, his eyes wide as he searched the room. His chest expanded with a deep breath when he saw me, and another button popped off his shirt. He stalked toward me with the predatory grace of a lion.

I barely had time to react before he lifted me into the air and captured my lips in a frantic kiss that stole my breath. His hands shifted from my waist to my butt and he lifted me higher. My long apricot-colored skirt pooled around my hips as I wrapped my legs around his waist. His lips gentled on mine, the tone and tempo changing to something softer. He pulled away, and I grunted in protest. He laughed and kissed the tip of my nose.

"I can't believe you wrapped me up in flowers," he complained, but his eyes were shinning with laughter. "And then left me."

I let out a breath, tension draining from me to see the light back in his eyes.

His expression turned serious when he cupped my cheek. "Dia, I've almost lost you twice now. Once to a maniac and once to my own stupidity. I'm sorry for shutting you out. I've been hiding my feelings for so long, it's become a natural reaction. I don't want to hide who I am anymore. Not from myself, and especially not from you. But I'm a work in progress. I'm trying to figure out how all of my pieces fit together." He brushed a finger down my cheek. "There is so much I regret now—hurting you most of all."

I brushed the hair back away from his face and pink petals fell to the ground.

"We all have regrets. My mother fought depression for most of my childhood. Some days she couldn't get out of bed. Even on her good days, she wasn't really all the way there with me." A tear trickled down my cheek. "I hated that she was so weak to let my father's leaving make her sick. She finally got help and became a great mother. But I promised myself I would never be like her. Now I know what she went through, and I'm so sorry that I resented her for all those years when she was hurting."

"You were a child, Dia. Don't beat yourself up over that. She was the only parent you had. It was her job to take care of you, not the other way around."

No, it shouldn't have been my job. But she had been grieving the loss of her eldest child and trying to raise another all by herself. Any lingering resentment I'd had toward my mother was gone. The first thing I planned to do when I got home was hug her and tell her how very proud I was of her. She had beaten back the darkness for me, and I was eternally grateful.

"I've forgiven her for that," I said. "And I forgive you too."

"You are the most amazing person." He stared at me in awe. "I wasn't looking for love, but it knocked me on my ass with a pink glitter picket sign. I never had a chance."

My mouth had gone dry, and for the first time ever I couldn't think of one thing to say.

"Well, now I know. Kissing you doesn't shut you up but telling you I love you does." He smirked, clearly amused that he had made me speechless. "You don't have to say anything. I know you've been through a lot. We'll take it slow—"

I slid my hand up around his neck and pulled his mouth down to mine. His taste overwhelmed my senses like a potent wine as we drank greedily from each other. His groan vibrated across my tongue as his hand slid up my thigh. *More.* I wanted his hands all over every part of me.

When I rubbed myself against the obvious bulge in his pants he hissed and pulled away. His beautiful midnight-blue eyes had that lighter blue ring around them again, and it was pulsing with the heavy thud of his heart. He held my thighs, keeping me secured to him, but kept our upper bodies as separated as possible.

"I thought you wanted me?" My old insecurities reared

their ugly head. I pushed against him, but he wouldn't let me down. "I get it. Ok, I'm not really your type. I don't have breasts the size of melons or that creamy white skin like Nikki. You don't want to be seen with a dirty gypsy girl, fine. Let me go."

"What the hell are you talking about?" Jaxon's eyes were wide in shock. "I told you I love you. I've never said those words to another person. How could you think I don't want every part of you? Every single inch of you is amazing. You're my exotic little Tigerlily. You're strong, smart, and so damn beautiful you take my breath away."

He pulled me against him and kissed my lips. "I want to be with you, Dia. I can't be near you without my heart beating out of control and my cock getting hard. But I won't be taking my brother's lead this time. I won't risk losing you again to lies or half-truths."

What truth did I need to know that could keep us apart? My heart was beating out of control. My stomach twisted in knots dreading what he might say. "What do you mean?"

"You are my mate. I knew I was incredibly drawn to you when we first met, but I knew for sure you were meant to be mine the first night on the island. Do you remember when we were in the throne room and our eyes met? I felt the Desmòs—the bond—form between us then."

I remembered he had risen from his chair like he had been electrocuted. "You looked horrified," I said.

"That wasn't horror, but terror. My bachelor days were officially over as of that moment." He chuckled, then his expression turned serious. "A bond-mate is sacred to the Paldimori. They are our other half, able to join with us in a connection so strong that we share everything. Our thoughts. Our powers. Our lives. I never expected to find mine. But here you are."

He pressed our hips together tighter and my breath hitched. "A bond-mate—when the link is fully formed—is the same as a wedding to the Paldimori. It is activated through sex. It means that if I get inside you, that's it. There is no going back for either of us. We will be connected for life and you will be my wife."

I gulped, trying to wrap my head around everything he had told me. Could I open myself so completely to someone? There could be no secrets in a connection that close. No place for either person to hide. "I'm scared," I whispered. "What I feel for you, there's no comparison. It's so big. I'm afraid it will swallow me up. I don't want to lose myself."

"I'm scared too." Jaxon brushed the hair back over the bare shoulder revealed by my tank top and kissed my nose. "I'm afraid of what you'll see inside me when we're joined. But I'm more afraid of losing you. I lost everything once, and it has loomed over me my whole life. I won't lose you. We don't have to do anything right now, we can take it slow. I'll take whatever you're willing to give me and cherish it. And I would be deeply honored if you decide to someday become my wife."

He meant that. He would really not have sex with me until I was ready to be his wife in every way that meant to his people—*our* people. I loved him even more for that. What did I want? When I looked past the fear of getting my heart broken again, all I found was a giddy joy that was ready to burst out of me like an exploding piñata.

Jaxon loved me. I had felt it in every gentle touch. He showed it every time he got all grumbly and protective. But most of all he showed that he loved me when he treated me like an equal. He asked what I wanted and let me make my own decisions even if he didn't like them. Jaxon gave me something Dan never had—respect.

"How do you feel about cats?"

Jaxon laughed and spun me around. "I will love your cat just as I love you." My heart skipped a beat when he said those words.

His eyes burned with a fierce heat as the light flared around the edges again. "You're sure? You'll be tied to me in every way possible. Heart. Mind. Body."

Every thought in my head was my own—now that I'd learned to block out the ghosts—and they were all filled with a future that was suddenly looking very bright.

"You already own all of those pieces. I love you beyond words and I don't want to wait to make you mine. Yes, I'll marry you—"

"—Jaxon Eros Baines. That's my full name. You'll need to know it for later. When I'm making you mine, forever."

The wind swirled around us as he sealed his lips to mine. My body felt like it had burst into a thousand shards and then was put back together. I tore my lips from his to find we were back in the pine meadow. "How ...?"

"Teleporting." He grinned mischievously. "I have a few more tricks I'll show you some time. Right now, I have other goals in mind."

He released my butt and let me slide down his body. My bare feet touched the ground and the grass felt like it hugged me. Jaxon grabbed my hand and spun me around until my back was to his front. He raised my arms up and pressed my hands to wrap around his neck.

"Hold on tight." He whispered, then we lifted off. My heart raced as we hung in the air several feet off the ground. Wind whistled through the caves in the cliff, filling the air with notes and I laughed. The wind was playing the *Aladdin* song "A Whole New World." Jaxon's hands trailed down my arms. Then down my sides where his fingers brushed the sides of my breasts. My laughter cut off as arousal tightened my nipples. "Give me your hand."

I placed my opposite hand in his and he spun me out. My skirt flew up around my hips. Then we were pressed together, chest to chest. One hand smoothed down my hip to my thigh and brought my leg up to wrap around his hip. His arousal pressed hot and hard against me. He dipped me back and placed kisses from my neck down to the top of my shirt. His fingers trailed up my thigh pushing my skirt higher. His mouth nuzzled against my breast as his fingers traced the outer edge of my underwear. My breath caught and held. Then released on a moan when his mouth closed over my breast through the fabric of my shirt and his hand cupped me.

"J-Jaxon, please," I shamelessly begged. It had never felt like this. Like every part of my body was focused on him and waiting eagerly for his touch. He pulled me upright, then sent me spinning out again. Ordinarily I would have loved to dance with him, but my body ached for his touch. I spun back to him and his smirk. He glanced down, and I followed his gaze.

How had he gotten my skirt off? Oh, there goes the underwear too. *Wind is a handy power.*

My eyes closed on a groan as cool air met my heated core. My hands gripped his biceps to keep my knees from buckling and he chuckled.

Oh, two could play at this game. I ran my hands up his chest and started unbuttoning his shirt. Then kissed each inch of tanned skin revealed. When he tipped back his head, I padded the ground below us with a thick bed of clover and surrounded it with red tiger lilies. I grew a soft vine from the ground and wrapped it around his ankle. I pulled his shirt off and tossed it aside. My tongue traced the low waist line of his jeans just before the vine yanked him to the ground. Jaxon landed on his back with an *oomph*.

I smiled triumphantly until he flashed me the most wicked looking grin I'd ever seen. Then I was flying through the air to hover right over top of him.

"Do you know what I've been wondering since our first meeting ..." Jaxon leaned up to capture my lips and my mind went blank. He pulled away, and said, "... If you taste like strawberry shortcake?"

I frowned at him in confusion. Then my eyes widened as the wind maneuvered me around, then dropped me with my knees on either side of Jaxon's head. He didn't waste any time putting his theory to the test. I shivered at the first slide of his tongue. Squeaks issued from my mouth as he gripped my hips and pressed me down so that there was nowhere to escape. Great Mother Goddess, the man was good with his mouth. Ecstasy unfurled within me, growing by leaps and bounds. Then bloomed into a riot of colors as I tipped over the edge.

I braced my hands on my knees as Jaxon placed gentle kisses on my thighs. The wind picked me up once more and laid me out over Jaxon like a blanket. I sighed as I rested my head on his chest and his fingers combed through my hair. I swirled my fingertips along his firm chest in random patterns to the beat of the song still being played by the wind. I traced his hipbone poking over the waist of his jeans, and he went still beneath me. I raised my head to look at him and the blue around his irises flared.

"What makes your eyes do that? It's beautiful."

"It's one of the signs of a bond-mate connection." My fingers brushed the bulge in his pants and he jolted. His voice was a hoarse rasp when he said, "Most only ever see the blue ring and that's enough. But you're Chosen and I'm powerful in my own right. I think our bond will be similar to what my brother has. When their connection completed, their eyes changed for a bit like looking into a kaleidoscope; at least, that's what I hear."

I was ready to find out. I cupped him and leaned up to kiss his neck. My hands made quick work of his zipper and I used the clover to help me tug off his pants. He pulled my shirt off and placed his hand against my heart. "I love you, Claudia King. Do you accept me as your bonded mate and husband?"

This was real—we were going to be husband and wife. "Yes, and yes a million times. I love you and accept you, Jaxon Eros Baines."

He pulled me down to capture my lips in a slow, sweet kiss. His hands payed homage to every inch of my body and I had never felt more beautiful in my life. Our lips parted, and I saw the same hunger in his eyes. I gripped him in my hand and placed myself over him. Slowly, I sank down. It was a tight fit and Jaxon watched me with feverish eyes as I slowly lowered myself. I was sure at any moment he would take control, but he never did. Finally, he was all the way inside.

Jaxon let out a choked sound when I raised up slightly and reseated myself. Sweat beaded his forehead. His hands gripped into fists at his sides. The blue ring around his eyes had started to vein out toward the center of his eye. My hips shifted up and down. At first slowly, while my body adjusted to him, and then faster. His hand unclenched to play with my breasts, and my hips jerked hard. We both moaned. He tugged on my nipples and it happened again.

"Oh gods, Dia, I don't know how much longer I can last," Jaxon panted. "But do that again. Gods, yes."

My core tightened and released, milking him. And sending me so close to the edge. "J-Jaxon, I'm ..."

"I've got you, always." He laced our fingers together and pulled me forward. Our eyes met only inches apart. The blue in his edged to purple, then green, and a dozen other colors. My heart lurched as the building tension snapped inside me and sprouted wings. Jaxon's cry joined mine, and I felt the warmth of his release inside me. A disco ball of colors played inside my mind. Suddenly, I could feel Jaxon there with me—his voice in my head.

"Body of my body," his voice whispered through my mind, "Soul of my soul. We are one."

23

Jaxon's bedroom lay at the top of the cliff underneath a clear glass dome. He had teleported us here after we made love in the pine meadow. He had certainly succeeded in making himself a fantastical landscape. The rocky cliff area I had stared up at was a honeycomb of twists and turns into various rooms. I knew what Molly had meant now when she threatened to send the servants to clean his rooms when we first stepped off the plane: someone could get lost in that cave system for days.

Here at the cliff top, the bed was surrounded by circles of different things to explore. One layer in from the hyacinths was a ring of white sand. Next was a pebbled stream fed by a waterfall at the back of the room. Finally, in the center, the round bed stood on a glass floor looking down into a library.

We had spent the last several hours exploring our new connection. Sending each other thoughts, feelings, and images. We'd talked about anything that came to mind. I'd told him everything about Meara. And how I was so hurt by Lia and didn't know what to do. He'd told me about growing up with Bennett. And confessed his determination to truly take his throne at Vēlos Castillo—the home base for the House of Arrows in Mexico—and lead his people.

Stars twinkled in the sky above as I traced my fingers along Jaxon's chest. The air was filled with the sweet scent of the thousands of hyacinths that dotted the outer edge of the cliff top. I snuggled deeper into his side, lulled by the sound of rushing water from the small waterfall. I had plans for the bathing pool at the base of the falls when I found the energy to move again.

"Ah, there's my favorite blanket." Jaxon shifted to pull me over his chest.

"Why do you have a library under your bed?" I asked.

"I started collecting books as I sought out leads about my family," he replied. "I don't sleep much most nights. My dreams are always chaotic, but I never remember them. That's why I chose to make my floor this way. I have my books close by and a warren of caves to explore. It helps to pass the nights."

The dome above was now open to the night, and the moon highlighted every toned plane of Jaxon's body. *Perfection*. His feeling of satisfaction filtered through our connection and I sent him a mental eye roll.

It was different having him in my head than Meara. I was relieved to realize that I could now tell whenever Meara was with me. There was this feeling of something other— like she was inside me but not truly a part of me. With Jaxon, we were one energy in two bodies. I could feel everything he felt without even trying, but I was still me. We could close the door between us if we needed privacy, but we were both finding the open connection comforting. There was no place for lies or deception. Only unconditional love and acceptance.

Jaxon's fingers traced his symbol on my back. His silky

voice floated through my head. "I've never been the possessive type before, but I like that you wear my mark. It's different than I'd expected— different than mine."

I loved the red winged-arrow mark that stretched across his back. I'd spent some time tracing it with kisses.

"What does it look like?"

His finger tapped the location of the symbol to the right of my spine. "The arrow rests against the base of the tree, its wings folded as if waiting."

I poked him in the side. "It better be waiting in line. I'm still learning the other two powers."

"That's just the impression that I get. You are the only person I've ever known to have more than one permanent marking. The bond-mate mark can exist alongside a House symbol, but when the bond is sealed, one replaces the other. You are special—as I've always known."

"Pffft." I blew a raspberry. The charming act might work on others, but I knew better. "You called me a psychedelic pint-sized menace-to-society the first time we met."

"You clobbered me with a sign when I complimented you."

"Complimented me? How is telling me you would love to see my hair spread out over your pillow a compliment?"

"I said '*beautiful*' hair—that was a compliment." He ran his fingers through my hair as if to emphasize his point. "And I was right. I do love seeing your hair spread across my pillows. In my defense, my brain was addled at our first meeting by the glare from so many orange sequins. Where in the world did you find those pants?"

"It took me weeks to sew those sequins on!" I poked him again.

"How very ... industrious. Were you planning to run away to the circus?"

"I think I would like it in the circus. The elephants are super cute. But if you insult my clothes again, Le Pew"—I stood up on the bed and raised my hands letting my earth power loose to form a thorny rose on each palm—"I'll surround your bed with a rose garden and play a game of avoid the thorns."

"Uh huh." His eyes roamed over my naked body distractedly. "Tell me again why you nicknamed me after a skunk? I think 'Rocks My World' is more appropriate."

I choked on a snort. "I'm never calling you that."

I bounced on the bed, loving the hunger that filled his eyes and the arousal that was lengthening against his thigh. This god of a man wanted me, imperfect body and all. "I said you were like Pepé Le Pew and I was Penelope Pussycat. You thought you were all suave trying to talk me into bed, and I was running away from the stench of those pick-up lines. It's so sad that you don't know who they are. I'm ordering up a cartoon marathon, stat."

That sexy smirk crossed his face, but I knew now that it was reserved only for me. "I think you were intoxicated by me from the first, but in denial."

"You just can't admit that your charm failed."

"Did it? I see I need to prove myself again." His hands slid up my legs. A breeze pulled the roses from my hands and sent petals raining down around us. Jaxon sat up, and his tongue touched my core. I whimpered. My knees buckled as he proved he really could rock my world.

24

It was the day of the competition. All of the contestants were once again lined up on the shore of the lagoon. This time, I was in a one-piece swimsuit that exposed my entire back to show off my markings. Dozens of blood-red rubies circled my neck and hung down from a point at my collarbone in an arrow shape. Layered webbing lined both sides of the slender arrow shaft giving it the effect of red and black feathers. More rubies dotted the intricate braids in my hair.

"Well, well, girlfriend." Nikki's perky voice called out. "I hear you scratched that bedpost up good."

I turned to find her walking toward me. Her swimsuit was an iridescent gray that looked like someone had cut an oval out of the front. The cutout arched high, exposing the undersides of her generous breasts and dipped low to her pelvis. Six strands of grayish-black stones spanned the cutout, and there was one large pendant set into the choker neck of the swimsuit. She looked ready for a runway, not a race.

"What?" I asked, sure I had misheard her. How would anyone know about my night with Jaxon?

"Honey, I know that glow well." She flashed me her blinding smile, but there was something in her eyes that had me slipping into my self-defense training. I would be ready for whatever or whoever came at me today. "Eros left my body tingling for days. What that man can do with his tongue, oh!"

"My Tigerlily, my wife." Jaxon's velvety voice filled my head. The wind wrapped around me in a hug. "I've never slept with her. You are the woman I love. The only woman that will ever be in my bed again. Don't let her get to you. She's trying to distract you from the Games."

"Sorry, Nikki, I won't be comparing notes. He's never touched you and he never will." I held up my left hand where a ruby-red ring circled my ring finger. "He's officially off the market."

Jaxon had removed the torque necklace from my neck last night. The one I had been given and told to never take off that first night of the Games. I'd watched in awe as he used his powers to pull the large ruby from the necklace. It had hovered in the air and started to change shape. The red flowed like silk shaping a beautiful crown. He had placed it on my head and kissed me until I'd forgotten my name. Then he had taken the crown and held it between his hands until it shrank down into the ring I now wore. Jaxon explained to me that the gems were actually the crowns that the gods and goddesses had made for themselves when they ruled on Earth. When they decided to leave, they gave the jewels to the leaders of each House to help protect their descendants. The Kyrion thought they had other purposes too, but no one knew for sure.

Nikki's face turned red. Her eyes blazed with fury. Her hands curled to claws at her sides. The water in the lagoon right beside us started to bubble. Over Nikki's shoulder I saw Devon's head jerk in our direction. He stalked toward us with a murderous expression. The water settled abruptly. Nikki's smile came back, if a bit forced. "I was just teasing you. Congratulations, honey, you are one lucky girl." Then she turned and walked away.

Devon gave her a hard look as he strode past her. When he stopped in front of me, I looked up to meet his furious stare. "What happened?"

"Nothing," I squeaked out. He was so intimidating.

His eyes narrowed. "Where is your necklace? The one you were not to take off."

"Uh, here." I lifted my hand to show him the ring.

His eyebrows slammed down over hard eyes. His head swiveled to where the Kyrion stood off to the side of the lagoon, and he marched over to Jaxon. Through our connection I listened to them argue about pulling me from the competition. From what I could understand, with my powers and connection to Jaxon I had an unfair advantage that wasn't allowed in the competition since it was designed to wake a Potential's powers. In the end, Jaxon won by telling Devon that they would be violating the rules of the Games if I were removed now—six contestants were always required.

My attention shifted to the six large stone archways with iron gates that now stood on the shore of the lagoon in front of every symbol etched into the ground. The one toward the middle was much larger than the others and more elaborate. The pillars were made of a strange gray material that seemed to shift from solid to translucent. The arch was carved with scenes of mists rising up to devour people or usher them to heaven. The metal of the gate doors formed twisting mists that looked like twin tornadoes.

Five Kyrion, all in gray robes, positioned themselves in front of the archways. The one they called Erebus, the

Kyrion for the House of Shadows, stood in front of the tallest gate. He made a gesture and all the Kyrion threw open their robes. Underneath, the men wore black leather pants with silky button up shirts in their House color. The women wore long leather dresses in their House colors. Jaxon winked at me when he caught me staring.

"*Leather pants, really?*" I teased him through our connection.

"*Do they make my ass look fat?*" He turned to the side, sweeping the robes out of the way so I could get a look.

My throat went dry. "Uh huh, they totally do."

He laughed, knowing it for the lie it was.

The moment was broken when Bennett walked between us to take his place. Jaxon rubbed the back of his head where I could feel Bennett had just telepathically slapped him.

Erebus lifted his hands and a breeze ripped through the area as each of the gates opened. Then it felt like the pressure had been released from the room as my ears popped and swirling clouds of mist appeared in each doorway. Gasps sounded from a few contestants. Even having experienced some of the powers of the Paldimori, I found myself staring with wonder.

Mist began to pour from the doorways and swirl around the Kyrion's feet. Erebus was the first to rise. A swirling tornado of mist lifted him up into the air. The top half of the tornado lengthened and broadened until Erebus was sitting upon a massive throne atop the tornado base. The other Kyrion joined him in their smaller thrones until they were all hovering high over the lagoon.

Erebus lifted his hand and everything stilled. "The House of Shadows welcomes you to the second competition of the Paldimori Games. Three times you will be tested.

Three times you will face the shadows. Darkness and light are two sides of the same coin. Which will claim you?"

That's it? Really? The man definitely did not have a career as a motivational speaker.

Jaxon chuckled. *"Erebus is a man of few words. Good luck, my Tigerlily. Each of the three times that you cross over into Thanatos will be a little harder. Don't linger; don't let anything distract you. Stay focused."*

A sound like a freight train whistle blasted the air, and everything was in motion again. Then we were off.

I ran through the archway and straight into Thanatos. Looked like my first challenge of shadow would come right away. I thought I heard someone whisper my name, but I ignored it. I ran straight ahead and into the water. The change from being in Thanatos to being back in the lagoon and the training area was so sudden I wasted valuable time getting reoriented. Luckily, I wasn't the only one.

I pumped my legs hard and managed to reach one of the tunnels in the top row of the practice wall. My smaller form quickly darted through to the other side, and I was well ahead of the others when I passed the small black buoys noting the end of the training area. I took a big breath and dived.

Lights flickered on as I made my way through the underwater crevice. There were only a few feet between me and the rock walls on either side. Several feet below lay only darkness, beyond the reach of the lights in the rock ceiling above. It was unnerving. My mind started trying to play tricks, making me think I saw movement in the dark beneath me.

I let out a breath and tried to calm my racing heart. It wouldn't be good to freak myself out down here. I started singing "Just keep swimming," in my head. Suddenly, the water around me started to churn. The lights directly above me shattered. Then the ones up ahead. I swam harder, hoping I was close to the opening we had been told about. Something wrapped around my foot. I kicked hard, but it wouldn't let go. My fingers scrambled to dislodge whatever had a hold on me, but only found water. The water tossed and turned me. My lungs burned. My arms were tiring.

Help me find light.

My power rushed out of me and searched. Purple dots of light appeared in my mind. I reached out with my power and pulled the light to me. Seconds later, a swarm of jelly-fish surrounded me, their purple light bouncing off the rough-hewn rock walls. I glanced down to see a swirling band of water wrapped around my ankle. I reached out once more, pushing at the water. A bubble opened around my head and I gulped in air. A column of water punched me in the stomach. My forehead smacked into the rock above, the pain making me lose my hold on the air bubble. Blood floated in front of me from the cut on my head. Another column of water came at me, but a dark shape knocked me out of the way.

Mikhail's wide eyes met mine from only a few feet away. Then the column of water pushed against him. He tried swimming away, but it pressed in from all sides. He sank further and further toward the darkness below. I pushed off the wall and went after him. Our hands reached out for each other, our finger tips grazed. The column of water bashed into his chest, his legs slipped into the darkness below. Something flashed like lightening blinding me. Mikhail's mouth opened in a silent scream. His body jerked violently, then he was pulled into the darkness.

No! He had tried to help me. I needed to go after him.

"*No!*" Jaxon and Meara shouted in my head.

"Get out of there," Jaxon demanded.

The water churned again, coming back for me. I used my power and the water propelled me toward where the opening should be. The jellyfish stayed with me until I saw light up ahead. I thanked them and left them behind as I swam for the opening ahead. I surfaced with a gasp and heard two more gasps behind me as others came through. Quickly, I swam to the edge of the pool and hauled myself out.

"Move it, Dia," Molly called out from several feet away, where she held Saam's reins.

"Help Mikhail," I gasped out. "Attacked. Pulled him into the dark."

Molly shouted out orders to the other guides, then turned to me. She silently handed me a set of clothes, then taped a bandage to my head. "I'm sorry, Dia. The Games have to keep going. We're bringing in divers to search. There's nothing more you can do for Mikhail right now. Go. Finish this."

"You can't be serious. You want us to keep risking our lives?"

"I want you to finish what you started." She glanced down at my ring. "For your people."

She surprised me with a hug, then stuffed me into a red T-shirt and harem pants. I struggled and tried to protest, but she was way more skilled than me. I was on Saam's back speeding toward the valley before I knew what happened.

"She's right, my Tigerlily." Jaxon's voice calmed me. "The Games are important, and they have to be played out, once started. Please finish this quickly and come back to me."

I wanted to turn this horse around and yell at Molly. But I didn't. I leaned over Saam's neck and let him run. We raced across the valley I had looked down on from my window so many times. The wind whipped by, chilling my wet skin. Luckily, the sun was shining brightly, and soon enough my clothes were drying. Or they were until we crossed a creek.

Saam's sides were heaving as we gained on Kade. We thundered up a slope and then down the other side. Saam made a leap at the last part of the hill that put us neck and neck. I had to give Kade credit: he rode like a madman. I was mostly hanging on for the ride.

The trail we were supposed to follow appeared about a mile in the distance. Molly had told me the path up the mountain was narrow. If I could get there first, no one would be able to pass until we reached the top. I snapped the reins, urging Saam on. He surged ahead, and we were in the lead!

We were feet away from the rocky path when lightning struck a tree next to me. I screamed as sparks flew and flames erupted. Saam reared, bugling in fear. I managed to cling to his back out of sheer terror. I was practically wrapped around the horse's neck as he spun and started racing back the way we came. My shaky hand brushed against his skin searching for a connection. I pleaded with him to calm. I sent him pictures of us playing in the horse meadow. He huffed out a breath, his stride evening out.

Nikki and Maya came into view only a few yards ahead. Chris was bringing up the rear. I got us turned around in the right direction and we galloped back to the trail.

Kade sat astride his horse at the base of the trail and called out, "Are you ok?"

"Yes, I'm fine." I breathed a sigh of relief that mentally talking to Saam had worked. "What are you waiting on?"

"You. I wanted to make sure you're alright." Kade took off his white cowboy hat and ran a hand over his short ginger hair. "That was mighty strange. There ain't a cloud in the sky."

The sound of riders approaching had us looking at each other anxiously "Go ahead. I'll catcha at the top."

"No, Kade. You made it here before me. You should go first."

"Ma'am, pardon my saying so, but you offer a much better view. Besides, I think you deserve to win one after the hell you've been through this week." His solemn eyes met mine, both of us thinking about what had happened to Mikhail. "You've got spirit, and you don't give up. I admire that." He put his hat back on and tipped it toward me. "Now, if you don't get goin', neither of us will be winnin' this thing. The others are almost here."

"Hey, Kade ..." My smile was wobbly, but I tried to keep the worry from consuming me. "... I'm going to make you eat my dust for calling me ma'am again."

"Yes, ma'am," he grinned back.

We started up the trail. It was much slower going. The path twisted back and forth up the side of the mountain. In some areas, it was barely a couple of feet across, and I gripped the reins nervously until we got past those parts. Maya had caught up and was right behind Kade. Nikki and Chris had struggled but were closing the distance.

The sky was a beautiful deep blue with big fluffy clouds passing over and offering the occasional break from the heat. Now that we were slowed down to a walk, I was sweating under the midday sun. What seemed like hours later, we heard the sound of water. The trail leveled out and followed a creek until we came to a waterfall. There didn't appear to be any other exits except for the way we came in.

Tall rock walls formed a hidden grotto. The water here was a bright blue surrounded by a carpet of bluebells on either side. Kade and I got down to walk around one side. The other three contestants went to the other side. There was supposed to be another gateway here that we could pass through. We had worked our way along our side of the area when Kade and I both seemed to arrive at the same conclusion—the door had to be behind the falls.

I raced to the falls, but Kade beat me there. The rock was slippery from the water, and I clung tightly to the cliff as we walked the narrow shelf edging around the wall to get to the falls. The ledge widened once we passed behind the curtain of water and found another archway full of the swirling mists. Kade wasted no time stepping through. I hesitated a moment, some instinct niggling at me. Suddenly, Meara appeared beside me, an eerie wail pouring from her mouth.

I pivoted and struck out with my palm. My eyes met the shocked blue of Nikki's before she snarled and swiped at me with a knife. I drove my arms forward to isolate her knife arm. Then pulled her toward me and locked her in an armbar. She struggled against me, and a blast of water nearly knocked me off my feet. My knee connected with her face, and she cried out dropping to the ground.

Chris came around the falls. His eyes wide behind his glasses when he saw Nikki laying on the ground with a bloody nose. He kept me in his sights as he walked over and crouched down beside her. A spiral of water detached itself from the waterfall and loomed menacingly over his shoulder.

I froze in place, not wanting to see another person get hurt. Chris helped Nikki to her feet. She swiped at the blood seeping from her nose and smeared it across her cheek. Chris kept her close as they edged toward the door to Thanatos. "P-Please, stay where you are. We don't want any trouble," he pleaded.

The spiral of water made stabbing motions at his back and my fists clenched. Just as they stepped through, a flash of pain slashed across my upper arm. I turned to block the spiral of water that was now wielding the knife, knowing I was already too late. Then, as the knife plunged toward my chest, Meara appeared again and pushed me through the archway.

25

I gripped my bicep as I stumbled forward into Thanatos once more. Meara had saved my life again. Having my own personal haunting was turning out to be a blessing. Sticky wetness coated my fingers when I pulled my hand away, and I watched as gray droplets fell to the ground.

I had previously thought maybe my attacker was Mikhail. After all, he had deliberately bumped into me during the swim races. To be fair, I had gotten in his way twice before he came after me. I could even possibly see how Maya might have been trying to take out the competition to make sure her calculations panned out. But looking back now, it made sense that it was Nikki. She was powerful. She had to be. Her powers were clearly linked to water, maybe lightning as well. She had given me poisoned water. The only thing I struggled with was why? My mind kept coming back to how she had reacted to my marriage with Jaxon. Was this all because she'd wanted him?

I moved cautiously through the gray mists expecting Nikki to attack again at any moment. Occasionally shapes would appear. If I ignored them, they disappeared again just as quickly, but if I stopped to investigate they became more solid. Now I understood why Jaxon had warned me about not getting distracted by what I saw. Once I saw the hut my mother had lived in. My college dorm. Dan's house. The school where I had worked. On and on it went with places from my past appearing through the mists.

"Daughter." The whispered word stopped me in my tracks.

A darker shadow moved through the mists. The closer it got, the more solid it became until the suit-wearing-man from Chaméni Elpída stood before me. He was only a few inches taller than me, yet his presence seemed to fill the entire space. He smiled and held out his hand like we were long-lost friends.

"Who are you?" I asked, keeping my distance.

His lips pursed, and he let his hand drop. "That is a fair question given this is our first official meeting. My name is Paden Aidos. I am your father."

"So, you're the man who abandoned my mother and used my sister. Then attacked their village. Maybe you made a donation that led to my birth, but you're not my father."

"I was not given a chance to be anything more. My only child—the only one I knew of—was taken from me when she was just a girl. I have searched for her all these years. Then I see you, who looks so very much like my Meara. Surely you can imagine my surprise. And my regret that I did not know of your existence."

"And the villagers? Do you 'regret' what you did to them?"

He waved his hand, and the mists parted. Green grass appeared in a circle around him. Color climbed up from his feet to reveal his charcoal gray suit with a navy-blue vest and tie. His wavy white hair was combed back from his face and brushed the collar of his suit coat. He had a well-trimmed white beard and piercing blue eyes very much like my own. The mists pushed back further, and I was in full color too.

"Now is that not better?" He gave me an expectant smile clearly looking for a reaction, but I refused to give him anything. His smile fell, and pain tightened his features for a moment. "You asked about the village. It is not what you think. If you but come with me, I can explain everything."

"*No, don't trust him!*" Meara appeared by my side.

Paden stared in shock at the ghost of his eldest daughter. After what I had learned of this man I had expected a cold tyrant ready to destroy everyone in pursuit of power. The man before me was a complete surprise. His emotions were raw and sincere. Utter despair leeched the color from his face and formed grim brackets beside his mouth. His fine-boned hand pressed against his heart as if he was holding it together. Tears trickled down his cheeks as he took a tentative step toward my sister.

"My Meara. So, it is true you died that day. I would not believe." He pulled a locket from his breast pocket, and Meara gripped my hand. "I never stopped looking for you. My daughter, I am so very sorry."

Meara sobbed, "Liar! You killed them. You killed *me*."

He flinched like someone had slapped him. "I would never harm you. I only wanted what was best for you."

"You lie!" Meara held out her hand, and the mists swallowed him up.

"What did you do?"

"You can't trust him, Dia. You can't trust any of the—"

Then I was falling.

"Oomph!" I landed face down on the ground. Grass brushed my cheek, its fresh scent tickling my nose.

Squinting against the bright sunlight, I saw two shapes rush past me. I was back in Sotirìa!

I scrambled to my feet, taking off after Kade and Maya. We raced over the gently rolling ridge top toward the castle in the distance. A central doorway that looked exactly like Erebus's gate appeared to be the only entrance. The oval base of the castle spanned the entire width of the ridge. The building split into dozens of cylindrical towers a couple of stories up from the foundation. They spiraled around each other forming a giant upside-down tornado that branched off into dozens of different funnels. Monoliths, like jagged teeth, randomly dotted the grounds in front of the castle.

The sun started to make its descent behind the castle, shadows of the towers inching across the ground toward us like needle-tipped fingers. I weaved through the monoliths, gaining on the other two contestants. I passed through one of the castle's shadows: it had that same viscous sensation as Thanatos. I was missing something here.

I stopped. My breath sawed in and out as I watched the sun sink behind the castle peaks. Erebus had said we would have three tests of shadow. I had completed two. Each of them had been actual doorways into Thanatos. The castle door was the obvious answer, but I didn't feel that beckoning sensation like I had with the others. I cast my senses out as Meara had taught me. Spirit and shadow were facets of the same power. If I could just tune my power to the right frequency ...

I closed my eyes and imagined holding the bluish-white cord of my spirit power. Slowly, I weaved in tendrils of gray from the castle's shadow. The cord absorbed the shadows, and they floated in the light like mercury.

"That's it! You're doing it, Dia." Meara clapped enthusiastically in my head. "You'll be able to open a portal to Thanatos whenever you want."

I grabbed one last shadow and fed it to the cord. Suddenly, I was outside my body looking at a very different view. The structure I had seen as the castle before was now an endless loop of shadows. The monoliths lay flat on the ground forming a simple block castle with two square turrets. At its center was a single monolith with a bluish-gray glow around it.

Stone Shadow Castle. The real castle was hidden in the shadows, and I'd found it!

I memorized the monolith doorway and opened my eyes. In the distance, I saw Maya trip Kade as they came to the door of the fake castle. Hopefully, Kade wouldn't fall for the trap, but I couldn't worry about that. He could take care of himself. I had a competition to win.

I jogged to the monolith doorway and lay my hand upon the cool stone. A bluish-gray light flared under my hand. The light started to spread out in jagged cracks along the stone. My senses tingled a warning. I pivoted, the kick catching me in the hip instead of my ribs. I dropped and rolled across the ground then quickly got to my feet.

Nikki glowered at me, filled with hatred. Dried blood crusted her swollen nose and was smeared across her cheek. "I think you broke my nose, you bitch."

"You were too perfect, anyway. Now you have character."

"I had to take a backseat with Lia, but you're all mine." She gave me her thousand-watt smile. "There's no one here to protect you now. Not that anyone cares if you die. Your best friend abandoned you again. You think Eros is going to be a faithful husband? That man is built for sex. He's probably fucking someone right now."

"Are you gonna talk me to death?"

"You think you're so smart. You have no idea what's coming." She kicked at me again, but I dodged it. "The Paldimori are weak and stupid. They've lost so much of their history, they don't even know they're doomed."

"What do you mean?"

"You'll see soon enough." Water shot from her hands and surrounded my head.

I tried to break the bubble, but it was no use. I ducked Nikki's fist, but a second caught me in the stomach. Precious air rushed out of my lungs. If I breathed in, I was dead.

Meara appeared behind Nikki and kicked the back of her knee. Nikki shrieked and went down. The bubble broke, and I gasped for air.

Nikki looked around for the source of her injury, but my sister had disappeared. I took advantage of her confusion and kicked out, contacting her shoulder. She grunted and rolled away before I could follow up with a punch. A stream of water hit me in the face. I tried to duck away, but it followed me. A punch landed in my kidney. Pain spread along my back, but I spun away to avoid another hit.

I opened my senses to Meara letting her be my eyes. Using my earth power, I pulled vines up from the ground and wrapped them around Nikki's legs. She beat at the vines trying to pull free. Meara plowed into her, taking her to the ground. The water stream broke apart into droplets that hammered at me from all sides. I reached out with my earth power again and pulled leaves from trees to build a shield.

"Finish the competition, I've got this!" Meara shouted.

I wrapped an extra layer of vines around Nikki, then sprinted for the monolith door. I pressed my hand against it, and the light snaked out. The whole monolith was covered with veins of light; then, suddenly, it exploded, and I was tumbling down.

26

I fell through layers of shadow worlds. The first I recognized as Thanatos, the swirling mists I had visited several times now. The next was a mountainous landscape where midnight black shadows spewed from geysers to coat the land like tar. Another was a muddy gray-brown lake where people moaned in agony as the thick water bubbled up around them like some horrible soup.

Finally, I hit the ground with a solid thud that rattled my whole body. I sat up with a wince and took in my surroundings. I had landed on a narrow island surrounded by a reddish-gray river of lava. I scrambled away from the edge as a bubble burst sending lava splattering along the shore.

I backed into something solid and turned to find a single tree growing in the center of the island. The branches held only a few sickly-looking leaves. The trunk of the tree had a feminine shape, like a woman with her arms raised. Sections of damaged bark ran like battle scars across her body. What drew my attention, though, was the symbol of a lotus flower upon her stomach.

I felt pulled to the tree and, suddenly, it all made sense.

Destiny had always been leading me here to this place, to this moment in time. I was standing at the edge of that cliff again, knowing that one step could alter the course of my life. Of everyone's lives. I could feel her now. That presence I had known all my life was weak and fading. Already her influence had diminished, and our world was in trouble. If I walked away, she would eventually cease to exist.

It all came down to this moment. What would I give to save her?

I reached out hesitantly placing the lotus on my palm against the one on the tree.

The ground shook. Lava erupted into the air. Green light enveloped the tree and then me. The separate cords of my powers writhed like snakes in my belly. They bit into me, sending their essence through my veins. It felt like a branding iron seared my back. Screams ripped from my throat until I was too hoarse to do anything but whimper. A sound like the beating of a heart filled my ears getting louder and louder. I dropped to the ground. Every inch of my skin shivered at the mere feeling of the air upon it.

Emerald-green eyes opened within the face of the tree above me. Branches reached out to cradle my limp body. My lips stretched wide in screams that were no more than a hiss as the rough bark slid against my sensitive skin. Color spread across the island. Vibrant green leaves unfurled from the tree's branches as I was lifted higher. Cracking sounds filled the air as the tree's roots were pulled from the fractured soil. Then the tree began to walk. Tears leaked from the corners of my eyes as each jarring step drove pain through me.

Bark began to peel from the tree to reveal snowy white skin. The branches melted down to become long golden hair. More bark crumbled to reveal plump red lips.

"Dia, at last, you have come."

My lips trembled, but no sound came. "*Can't. Pain.*"

"I hear you, my child. Birth is always painful. Yet, I would have spared you if I could."

"*Dying.*"

"Death is but a kind of birth."

"*Not same.*"

"That is your human teaching. You have much to learn of your true nature. You are a daughter of my blood. Marked by the lotus as one of my warrior handmaidens. You are destined for much more."

"*Know you. Spoke to me.*"

"*Your family calls me the Great Mother. You may call me Gaia.*" Her face was now fully human and stunning as she smiled down at me. A yellow butterfly appeared like a tattoo on her cheek. Then lifted off and flew away. "*I have not taken this form for many centuries. But I am always near for those who know where to look.*"

"*You watching?*"

"Always. The world is mine to protect. It spoke to me even in my slumber. But it became harder to react when she called." Her brow furrowed in worry. "We chose to slumber and wait for the day when the prophecy would be fulfilled. Yet we did not know the toll it would take. It is nearly too late."

The branches lowered. Out of the corner of my eye, I could see the lava lake below.

"*My family? Meara? Jaxon?*"

"They are safe, for now. Your sister is here. I am blocking her, as I am Jaxon. In Meara's fear for you, she might do you harm. Not deliberately, but she is not in control at the moment." Her gaze dipped to my shoulder. "You both bear the mark of Hades. His power is much stronger in her, and she is untrained."

The heat of the lava reached out for me. My shallow breaths struggled even harder as the heated air seared my throat.

"Promise. Save them."

"I cannot make that promise, my child. Some things are destined. Others are still to be written. The rules of the Games have been broken. The future is more uncertain than ever."

The branches began to weave together around me until only my eyes were left uncovered. I tore feebly at the rough bark. I wasn't ready to die. Gaia bent over me, her body now fully human looking except for her arms. *"Do not fight it, Dia. There is a purpose in all that has happened and all that will happen."*

Then the branches covered my view. Dirt seeped through the cracks between the branches making me cough. Soon I was packed in tightly, with only a shallow pocket of air around my face. My heart was racing. My breaths were rapid and shallow. My stomach rolled with a queasy certainty that this was to be my grave. Some niggling thought was trying to break through, but I was too panicked to focus. The dirt piled up to my chin and filled my ears. What was I forgetting?

"... call me Eros and I will answer ..."

"Eros! Jaxon!" I screamed mentally and verbally, just as the dirt covered my face. Then I was falling into the lava below.

27

"How many this time?" Gaia asked.

"It is hard to say, my lady. The attacks were widespread." It was my lips that moved, but the voice that came out was deeper. "The Dalton tribe were hit hardest. There were no survivors."

Where was I?

I was looking at Gaia from an equal height. That meant I definitely wasn't in my own body. We were in a giant room with rough-cut stone walls. Six black thrones sitting to one side were the only things in the room. It appeared to be a crude version of the Tower Room where I had pledged myself to the House of Arrows.

A bone-deep cold settled in. One I recognized. This wasn't a dream. I was inside another ghost.

"Was it the same as last time?" There was an intense green glow around Gaia that pulsed brighter.

"An elder from a local tribe confirmed." The woman I was in hesitated a moment, her thoughts full of anger. "A child had been born a fortnight ago who bore the marks."

Gaia closed her eyes and reached for the woman's hand. The hand that met hers was covered in scars. The fingers were much *longer and calloused than mine. And surrounded by that same green glow.*

"Two years, Alena." Gaia gripped the woman's hand tighter. "It has been two years since we first learned of the other ship of survivors. Yet we have only been able to rescue a handful."

"Mother, it is not your fault." Alena placed her hands on Gaia's shoulders. "You cannot take on the weight of all our problems. Especially this one. The survivors are not easily found. They scattered like the wind and have become good at hiding amongst the humans."

"Yes, that is true. But we have failed them nonetheless. My daughter, you are a fierce warrior, but you know little of politics." Gaia smiled and patted her cheek. "There is always blame to be laid. I have assumed the leadership of the Order. As the leader of my handmaidens, you know that means that fault is always yours to own."

Alena bowed her head, her thoughts a mixture of pride and resentment at this truth. "Why you? Why must you lead?"

Gaia sighed and turned toward the empty thrones. "Chaos united us for so very long. Without him, nothing is the same. But the Order is still here. Our purpose is—as it always was—to bring balance to this world. We cannot do that if we cannot stop fighting amongst ourselves. We need a leader. Eros and I are the strongest." Her fingers laced tightly together. "But something happened to him when he went to find Lyannìa. He will not speak of it with anyone, but I have seen the haunted look in his eyes when he thinks no one is watching."

Her fingers tightened until her knuckles turned white. "We are hunted. Sotirìa keeps us hidden and safe. But the others lost to the human world have no defenses. They must be found." She looked at Alena with tears in her eyes. "I cannot put this burden on Nikomedes. He is the most powerful Paldimori we have ever seen. Yet he is a seven-year-old boy. One who has been trauma-tized by the deaths of his parents."

Alena shifted nervously. "The Order has trained him hard these past years. Nikomedes is well-loved, and the people would unite around him. The fighting amongst ourselves might stop if he were to take his seat."

"You can see our powers like an aura surrounding us," Gaia said. "Tell me what you see when you look at the boy."

A shiver raced down Alena's spine. "A swirling wall of colors. And the shadow moving within."

Gaia nodded. "Nothing has changed?"

Alena shook her head.

"It is his connection that worries me." Gaia sighed. "I love Nikomedes like a son. I swore to protect him and train him. Yet I fear I have failed in this too."

"Mother, I may not know politics, but I know battle strategy," Alena said confidently. "Nyx will always argue because it is you she opposes. Tartarus would see himself king, if only to claim more land. Erebus is content in the shadows, as always. Eros, well, we both know he is distracted." She started talking faster, exited by the chance to do something more. "Nikomedes has gotten better. He is talking now. Set him on the throne. Let him be the voice by which you speak. Use his powers to find the lost and bring them home. Use his powers to fight back."

Gaia waved her hand dismissively. "Alena, I cannot use him like a common weapon. He is a child."

"Mother, he is both. His power is unmatched, even by you. Why are we keeping our best weapon out of this fight?"

Gaia walked away and slumped onto her throne. "Do not ask this of me."

"I can do this." A thin boy appeared beside Gaia's chair. His wavy black hair hung past his shoulders. Big sapphire-blue eyes stared up at Gaia, their depths full of knowledge, far too old for a child his age. This was the same boy I had seen before. When I thought I was having a dream, I must have been in Alena's head then as well.

"Nikomedes, how many times have I told you it is not polite to use the shadows to spy on others?" Gaia admonished in a soft voice.

"Many times," he stated. "But how would I know what is happening if I do not listen?"

"He has a point, Mother. He is a member of the Order after all."

"Daughter, you go too far." Gaia slammed her hand down on the arm of her throne, and the room shook. "We swore to protect all children, even one as powerful as the son of Chaos."

Gaia's expression softened as she turned to Nikomedes. "Your father would be proud of your bravery and dedication to our people. One day, you will make a fine leader. But you need time to be a child. You need time to heal."

Nikomedes placed his small hand upon her arm. "I m-miss mother and f-father. I wonder at night"—his throat worked, and tears slid down his pale cheeks—"what my s-sister would have been like if she had l-lived. My friends d-died. So many people died. But I lived. I have asked why, but n-no one answers. If my powers will s-save the lost maybe that is why."

Tears slipped down Gaia's cheeks as she gathered the frail-looking boy to her. "If this is the purpose you need to heal, then I will gladly stand by you. It takes more strength to live even when it seems like all hope is lost. Never doubt you are destined for greatness, and you are strong enough to survive anything."

The black-and-red dragon dropped into the room from an opening in the ceiling. It flapped its mighty wings and landed in front of the thrones. In the blink of an eye, Nikomedes was sitting upon its back.

As if called, the other members of the Order appeared upon their thrones.

Nikomedes's eyes swirled with colors as he raised his small fist into the air.

"We fight!"

28

It was the pain that woke me. Raised voices stabbed through the darkness like spikes straight into my head. My throat worked convulsively as I sucked in gasps of air that burned all the way down. Where was I?

"... there was no sign of a heartbeat. We have been trying to get in, but nothing has been able to penetrate the lava rock."

"Move aside, boy, before I lose my patience. Do you not know what the markings on her palm mean? Dia is the first handmaiden in over five hundred years. Anyone with half a connection to the Goddess felt her ascend."

"Mami, you must calm down. Your heart—"

"My heart is fit and fine. I'll not have this upstart think he can keep me from my granddaughter."

"Elder Rosella, please, our connection was lost—" Jaxon's voice choked off. "If she is alive, you have to tell me."

I wanted to shout out to tell them I was here, but nothing came out. My hands felt around in the darkness and brushed up against bark on all sides. Panic struck, my heart flopping in my chest like a beached fish. I was trapped.

Grandmother's voice softened, "The Goddess's ways are not always gentle, child, but a warrior has to be forged in fire. Use your bond and see for yourself."

"*Dia ...!*"

"*I'm here. I'm alive,*" I shouted into our connection. Jaxon's emotions spilled into me. A tangle of fear, love, and relief mixed with my own.

"*I thought I'd lost you.*" Phantom fingers traced my cheek. "*Our connection was severed. What happened?*"

"*I met the goddess, Gaia.*"

A furious familiar voice made me lose my train of thought.

I gulped down a sob. "*Is that Lia?*"

"*Yes, she's here. And in rare form,*" Jaxon chuckled.

That must be the raised voices I heard. *She came back!* was the thought that sparked a second burst of happiness in my chest. That was followed by a less happy thought. Lia in a rage was not something that should be witnessed by small children—or anyone, really. She was about to go supernova on my "egg," and I didn't want to get fried. A goddess had already set me to boil in a lava pit. All because I had woken her up. I thought I was the world's worst morning person, but she defiantly got that title. Sheesh!

Dirt shifted around me as I lifted up to push against the barrier above. My stomach rolled as pain knifed through my back, but I didn't stop.

I winced as Grandmother and Lia took jabs at each other. "*Oh, those two are going to be fun,*" I said to Jaxon.

"*I'm enjoying having your grandmother aim her crotchety ... I mean, sparkling personality at a new target.*"

"*Good save.*"

"*Thanks, I'm practicing for the future.*" He sent me a picture of him in a full suit of armor as our families were seated around Thanksgiving dinner. My grandmother was shooting rocks at him from a slingshot while his sister carved the turkey with a twisted smile. "*Although I think my homicidal sister trumps your crazy grandmother.*"

I laughed and finally the pressure that had been building up in my chest eased. "*I want a future with you. Even with the nuts in our family trees.*"

"*Then you better get your beautiful butt out of that rock.*" Heat filled me as his hands brushed over my naked body. "*I know just how to celebrate your 'hatching.'*"

"*Didn't you hear my grandmother? I'm a bad mama-jama warrior now. You best stop distracting me.*"

A phantom kiss pressed against my lips. "*Yes, you are. Come back to me, Tigerlily. I need you in my arms.*"

My focus shifted to the powers at my center. There were no longer three distinct lights, but a blended swirling mass. I sank into the mass and let it fill me. Light shot through my veins, filling every corner. The bluish-white was my spirit power. The red was my shared power with Jaxon. The green my earth power and my connection to Gaia.

Newfound confidence grew in me like a sapling that was finally being nourished. All I had to do was believe in myself, and I could do anything. I opened my eyes. The darkness was never going to take me because I carried the light inside. That's what I had been missing. It wasn't colorful clothes or happy paintings that kept the dark at bay —it was me. I could see my people clearly through my connection to Gaia. They were scattered and scared. My tribe had named their home Chaméni Elpída—Village of Lost Hope. They weren't the only ones who had lost hope. But I would teach them, and we would restore that hope together.

I understood now what my purpose was. The House of

Seasons needed to be rebuilt. Not only with select individuals that were strongest, but with all descendants of the Goddess. We were one tribe. The earth was ours to protect, and she was sick. The pollution and destruction were like dark sludge staining the Earth. I could see it all so clearly.

We would gather the tribes and start with what we could fix. Once we had helped repair some of the damage to our home, it would be time to meet with the other Houses to plan. Our enemy knew us better than we knew ourselves, but that was going to change. War was coming for us all.

My fist shot through the barrier above me. My fingers gripped the edges of the hole as fresh cool air seeped in. With a pulse of my powers, the egg started to dissolve around me like melted wax. I floated up from the remains. Then dropped to the ground in a crouch at the edge of the lagoon where the competition had first started.

Lia gasped, "Good god, she's like the Terminator."

My body was corded with new muscle. When I stood, I could tell I was a few inches taller. My eyesight was so clear I could see the individual hairs on Jaxon's arms from ten yards away. My ears picked up a whispered conversation two guides were having at the edge of the forest halfway across the training area.

"*You hear what the trees hear,*" Meara said gently in my mind. "*Are you ok?*"

"I think so." The pain had receded and left me with this new body to get to know. This would take some getting used to. "*Are you? I thought I had lost you for a minute.*"

"*Gaia gave me a choice, but I couldn't leave you. Sisters stick together.*" Her cold presence brushed against my thoughts like a butterfly kiss. "*And you still need me.*"

"*I should be mad at you for not moving on, but I'm selfishly glad you didn't."* I pulled my hair over my shoulder to hide as much of my nudity as possible.

Gasps echoed around the cavern.

"See how the House of Season's symbol has changed?" Grandmother clapped her hands. "The Goddess has been restored."

Jaxon stalked toward me like a dangerous predator. His eyes locked with mine, their deep blue depths sparked with the hunger of possession. He pulled a robe out of thin air and wrapped it around me. Using it to pull me into his chest, he crashed his mouth down on mine. His taste filled me like rain nourishing the ground after a long drought and my world felt a little more right.

"I didn't think it possible, but you are even more beautiful," he said gruffly through our connection. *"You, my little Tigerlily, are in trouble. You died."*

I looped my arms around his neck, the movement was much more comfortable with my new height. *"Lucky for us both this curious cat has a goddess on her side."*

"To hell with the gods and the prophesy." Jaxon gave me a fierce look. *"You are my life. Where you go, I go. No more adventuring without me."*

"Together. I like the sound of that."

"Good, because I'm never giving you up."

How was it he always knew just what to say? *"I'm not giving you up either, Le Pew. I love you."*

"I love you, my Tigerlily." He cupped my cheeks and kissed me until my head spun.

"Ouch!" Jaxon let me up for air but didn't let me go. My grandmother aimed her cane at his shin again, but he put me in front of him.

I laughed when grandmother winked at me. "How are you feeling, child?"

I paused a moment to take inventory. "Weird, but strangely like I'm finally myself."

"Trust the Goddess." She patted my hand. "Your transformation is for a higher purpose. She has given you the tools to succeed. Now the rest is up to you."

"Your symbol has changed." Jaxon's fingers traced the pattern under my robe. "The tree's branches are full of leaves now. The figure of the woman in the trunk of the tree is more obvious. She now holds my symbol—the winged arrow—in her hands. And at her feet sits the mark from your father's house—the three-headed dog of Hades. It seems you have been triple-blessed by the Gods."

"The prophesy foretold of the return of the Kòri." Light green eyes glowed from the darkness of the woods. Then the Kyrion of the House of Seasons stepped into the light. She floated across the meadow toward us, a wooden staff with ancient writing gripped in her hands. "And here she is. The Goddess has given us a powerful warrior. We have much to do if you are to restore the Spirit of our people."

29

Jaxon had declared that I wasn't doing anything else but going back to our rooms so he could hold me in his arms. We had both been through so much that I didn't argue. We had made love for hours and talked late into the night. There was still so much for us to learn about each other, but the more I learned, the more deeply I fell in love with him. Like the fact that my husband was hiding a lot of brain power behind that sexy smile. He had used a small sample of my blood that had been spilled when I was first claimed by the Goddess to test against the tribe. He was able to confirm that I had several close relatives, including an aunt, among them.

The sneaky man had also been in contact with my mother and already introduced himself as her future-son-in-law. He said he was hedging his bets to make sure there was no out clause for me to use. He had been smart enough to tell me that while kissing his way down my stomach. I had been too distracted to yell at him, but I would make him suffer for that later. I'm not sure how my mother was going to handle the fact that I had found our tribe or that I was married to a Kyrion. She wanted a normal human life for me, and now I understood why. Telling her about all of this was not going to be fun. I had faith that whatever happened we would get through it.

Jaxon had also tracked down information about my father. We would be going through the files he had put together later. I had spent my whole life wondering about the man who had walked out on his family. I wanted to hate him for a lot of reasons, but I couldn't. He really had loved Meara. I was telling myself someone who loved that much couldn't be all bad. Only time would tell.

Something tickled my nose. I swatted it away and rolled to my side.

Lips pressed down my spine causing me to wriggle away. "Closed," I mumbled into my pillow. "Pretty. Sleep you."

Jaxon chuckled as he rolled me over and pressed a kiss to my nose. "You are adorable when you are all sleep-confused."

My hands waved about trying unsuccessfully to push him away. "Mmm. Not."

"Yes, you are." He pressed kisses to my cheeks. "And absolutely irresistible. Don't think I'll be letting you out of this bed for a very long time."

My grumbling turned into a squeak when his tongue traced a circle around my naked breast. When he took my nipple into his mouth, heat shot through me and my back arched off the bed.

"Do you know what I love about the changes to your body?" he said. "It gives me an excuse to refamiliarize myself with every inch of you."

Not that he needed an excuse—he was just an opportunist. His hands flowed across my muscled belly and down to my hips. Suddenly, I was flipped onto my stomach. "I'm buying you yoga pants in every color imaginable."

"It's bigger, isn't it?" I groaned as he massaged my butt. "You know I'm not going to do Downward Facing Dog every time you want to enter a room, right?"

"Shhh, don't take away my dreams." Jaxon squeezed my butt cheeks and pulled me back against his hardness. I bit the pillow, my center still so sensitive from the many times we had come together last night. The connection between us was wide open, feeding me every sensation he felt which doubled my pleasure.

Slowly, he sank inside me as he stretched his body out over mine. My breath caught and held. Then stuttered out on a shaky exhale as he linked our fingers and began to move. We moved together in perfect harmony as we slowly built to a crescendo.

My skin was slick with sweat, my hair plastered to my back when I finally lost my patience. Using one of my self-defense moves, I knocked Jaxon off me and pinned him to the bed. He laughed up at me with light blue rings of light pulsing around his eyes. I placed my hand over his heart, our connection buzzing between us even stronger. When I slipped over him, it was his turn to gasp as I set the pace that tipped us over the edge.

Starlight burst behind my eyes. The colors of our powers swirled around the room. Every part of us was one at that moment as we shared feelings of bliss and a love so strong no words could ever do it justice. I snuggled into his arms, listening to his heart beat.

There was some part of me that had still been clinging to my old life, but, at this moment, I knew that Port Lawson would never be my home again. My home was wherever

Jaxon was. I had found the love and family I had always wanted.

Lia and I were talking to each other again. It was going to take some time to build back our friendship, but we would get there. It was also going to take some work to keep Lia, my grandmother, and Jaxon from killing each other, but I was up for the challenge. It would never be dull that's for sure.

As for Nikki, she had escaped. Turned out her background was all fake. Jaxon was working on it, but I didn't think he was going to find her. She really had been an amazing actress to have fooled us all. The more troubling part was how she had gotten into the Games to begin with. When I had told the Kyrion what happened, they'd claimed that there hadn't been a descendant of the six Houses with such strong water power in centuries. They had all stared at Molly, and she had stormed from the room. I knew that Molly had water powers and hoped that this new discovery wouldn't bring my new friend trouble.

Thinking of water powers brought to mind the other bad news we had gotten. I swallowed thickly and Jaxon held me tighter as sadness filled me. Mikhail's body had washed up on the beach the morning after the competition. I convinced the Kyrion not to wipe anyone's memories of him. Everyone deserved to be remembered. We had held a small ceremony for him last night.

Now we were down to three contestants, since I was no longer allowed to compete.

The Kyrion were calling an emergency meeting to discuss what to do. There were only three months left in the year. No one seemed to know what would happen if the Games weren't finished in time, but they all agreed it would be bad.

But for me, my mind was a much quieter place, and focus came more easily. My body was strong enough to be the warrior that my people needed—not just Gaia's descendants but all of the Paldimori.

Being a warrior had never been part of my plans, but destiny sets us on our course for a reason. The fight was coming, and we would be ready.

EPILOGUE

I woke to an anxious Jaxon sitting on the edge of our bed. "I was starting to worry," he said.

"I'm fine." I stretched and gave him a sleepy smile. "Getting transformed from a troll into an Amazon takes it out of a girl."

His lips brushed mine. "As much as you're tempting me to crawl back into this bed with you, we have somewhere to be."

"Don't I get a day off for being a good little descendent?" I grumbled.

"No rest for the sexy," he said with a smirk.

Then he scooped me up and kissed me breathless. When he set me on my feet, my knees threatened to buckle. He quickly ushered me out of our room before things could heat up. Moments later, he groaned when I stepped out of the bathroom in my camisole top and peach leggings covered in kittens playing with balls of yarn.

My step had a little more bounce to it as I walked toward him. I wasn't back to the same old me, but I was ok with that. The changes were here to stay, and I would adjust with time.

A few minutes later, we stepped out of the elevator into the Emerald Rain Forest. Phil waved a giant claw as if saying hello—my bright yellow bra wrapped around his head like ear warmers.

"Looking good, Phil," I called out to him. "Good thing I hate bras. I don't think I'm ever getting that one back."

Jaxon wrapped his arms around my waist, his hands resting dangerously close to my breasts. "You never have to wear those torture devices again."

"You're all for my comfort, huh?" I jumped when his hand slid higher to brush against me.

"Completely." He kissed the side of my neck then took my hand to pull me into the forest. "Panties are very restrictive too. We should probably remedy that."

"Forget it. I'm not going without underwear, Le Pew."

"I'm only looking out for your health." He gave me an innocent smile over his shoulder.

I grunted and focused on not falling on my butt as we picked our way through the thick growth. Jaxon still had a few inches on me, but, for once, I wasn't struggling to keep pace with his long strides. Although the changes in my body were taking some time to adjust to, my new affinity with nature was easing my way. Tree branches that would have smacked my taller height moved out of the way on their own. Tangles of weeds and rocks that would have tripped me up, smoothed into flat land.

This I could get used to.

We came to a clearing where a stone temple stood. Monkeys swung from vines that had grown all around the six oval-shaped buildings that fanned out from a central statue. An emerald statue of Gaia towered over it all. Her hands held a red lotus in each palm. Her white eyes glowed in the dim evening light.

The monkeys' chattering stopped abruptly as we neared the steps to the temple. They began to line up along the roofs, their white chests making them easy to spot in the dying light. Dozens of cinnamon-colored eyes tracked our every movement. Several bared their teeth at us, looking ready to attack. Jaxon kept walking as if he didn't have a care in the world.

"As much as it pains me to say this, your grandmother was right. We have forgotten too much of our past," Jaxon said. "We had no idea this was here."

Jaxon tugged me in front of him at the base of the steps. "Elder Rosella said this is the original temple where the Kòri—Gaia's warrior handmaidens—came to pay her tribute." He nudged me forward. "I'm not as good at using the Shadows as some, but I was able to check a couple of the buildings earlier. I couldn't see a way in. I have a feeling you may be more successful."

Oh great, he wanted me to be monkey bait.

"Uh, I doubt these monkeys are the cuddly *Curious George* kind. The big one over there is looking at me like I'm a huge banana."

"You're a Kòri. You have power over more than the trees and dirt." He gripped my wrists and turned my hands over. The lotus flowers on my palms sparkled like they had been traced in glitter. "The Kyrion are now actively pursuing all sources that might gain us knowledge of our past. I'm hoping you'll be able to find some answers here, not just for you but for all of us."

"Right, one monkey-tamer coming up." A piece of vine broke off and slithered toward us like a snake. Jaxon jumped when it twined around our left wrists. "And her trusty assistant. Too bad I don't have a pink bustier to put on you."

Jaxon leaned into me and whispered in my ear. "I won't wear a bustier, but you can tie me up any time. Just remember that I believe in fair treatment, so I'll be returning the favor."

My breath hissed out, and I practically ran up the steps to keep myself from dragging him back to our room. The man was more addictive than candy, and he knew it.

My earth power spiraled out with very little coaxing as we came to the base of the statue. The ground trembled, and a mound of dirt shot us up into the air. Jaxon lost his balance and fell over the side. The vine around our wrists held tight dragging me down too. I hit the narrow landing at the top of the dirt column knocking the air from my lungs.

Jaxon scrambled for purchase as he tried to pull himself up. My shoulder felt as though it was being pulled from its socket as I struggled to hold his weight. Jaxon used his power to raise himself up, but before he could make it to the ledge, a gust slammed him against the column of dirt. My own powers surged with my panic, and the column of soil plummeted.

Vines slithered about in all directions. Trees swayed. Rocks tumbled around the clearing crashing into everything. A swirling mass of mists hovered in the air. The monkeys screeched and took to the vines to swing around us like hairy acrobats.

"You've got to calm down!" Jaxon shouted. "Focus on pulling the energy back."

He grunted as he slammed into the side of the dirt column again. My heart skipped a beat seeing blood trickle down the side of his face.

One of the larger monkeys grabbed Jaxon's leg. He tried

to shake it off, but it held firm. Another monkey grabbed his other leg. To my surprise, they pulled him up onto the landing with me. I threw my arms around him. The jungle went still as I tugged the energy back with all my strength.

"Are you ok?" My fingers traced below the cut on his head.

"Just a scratch." It clearly wasn't, but if he was joking then he couldn't be too damaged. My sigh of relief was captured by his lips. "My powerful little Tigerlily, you were using all of your powers at once. You tugged so hard on our connection, I was having trouble controlling the wind." He winked at me when heat scalded my cheeks. "I can see we have our work cut out for us. Lucky for you I'm a very hands-on instructor."

My head settled against his chest, and I took a deep breath. My body wasn't the only thing that changed. My powers were much stronger now. I couldn't trial-and-error my way through this any longer.

"We'll figure this out together." Jaxon's hand smoothed over my braid. "As much as I love having you on top of me, we have an audience."

My eyes opened to find the big monkey that had helped Jaxon staring at me from only a foot away. It tilted its head as if listening to something, then started slapping the back of one hand into the palm of his other.

"Do you speak monkey?"

"I'm afraid this is your area of expertise."

We got to our feet. The monkey suddenly jumped from the dirt ledge to the arm of the statue. It mimed the hand motion again.

"I think it wants me to do something with my hands."

"I have a few ideas," Jaxon smirked.

"You're impossible, Le Pew." I nudged him out of the way

and stepped up to the outstretched hands of the statue. I glanced at the symbols on my palms then placed my hands in the center of the lotus flowers the statue held. Green light flared. The sound of stone sliding against stone filled the area. The oval-shaped buildings below us shifted until they interlocked to form a lotus shape.

The voice of the Goddess filled my head.

"The Kòri were my most trusted children. You will find answers in their temple, but not all knowledge is yours to gain. Time grows short, and the six are still scattered. Let faith guide the spirit, and you may yet succeed."

ACKNOWLEDGMENTS

Thank you to the small, but mighty, Callahan Clan Street Team who cheer me on and I know I can rely on for honest feedback. You all are awesome! Lee, April and Tiffany you ladies especially always go above and beyond.

Thanks to my wonderful editor who has made a world of difference on this book and is helping me grow as a writer.

Thank you so much to you, the readers, who purchased this book. With you all things are possible. I look forward to many more book journeys together.

ABOUT THE AUTHOR

T.L. Callahan is the author of the fantasy romance adventure series Paldimori Gods Rising. She has always been a book lover; devouring romance, fantasy, and poetry since she was a young girl growing up in Kentucky. Her love for the outdoors inspired hours of wandering the woods pretending to be on adventures discovering magical creatures and being the heroine of her own stories. That hasn't changed much these days. Never knowing what you can find around the next corner keeps her seeking out new adventures from backpacking in the Wind River Range of Wyoming to piloting a sailboat down the Tagus River in Portugal. T.L. lives in Ohio with her husband, son, and a cat that thinks he's a dog.

www.ingramcontent.com/pod-product-compliance
Lightning Source LLC
Chambersburg PA
CBHW071854220626
47052CB00002B/120